C000066780

AFTER TOMORROW

JACQUELINE HAYLEY

JACQUELINE HAYLEY
Love at the end of the world.

Reader warning: This series is set at the end of the world, so you can expect violence, gratuitous swearing and sex scenes that will make you blush. *you're welcome*

*Oh hey there, Jane Phillips. This one is for you. *blows kiss**

ACKNOWLEDGMENT

This novel was written on Wiradjuri Country in Central West NSW, Australia. I would like to acknowledge the Wiradjuri people who are the Traditional Custodians of the Land, and pay my respects to the Elders both past and present.

THANK YOU

With thanks to my beta reading babes, H.M. Hodgson, Tanya Nellestein, Heather McCarthy and Kelly Gay.

Heather and Tanya, I couldn't do this without you x

CHAPTER ONE

DAY 61

The apocalypse had its advantages.

A lack of internet, postal services and, quite possibly, all the people who worked in finance, meant no one was going to be bothering Kat Tenor about overdue credit cards any time soon.

She ran a hand through her shaggy pixie cut and grinned at herself in the age-spotted mirror on the wall. She didn't miss the instant despair that came with checking her online bank balance the morning after. And the amount of alcohol consumed last night would definitely have meant a diet of ramen noodles until her next pay.

"What time did you get in?"

Kat turned to find her best friend Chloe Brent-Maxwell awake and yawning. Flopping down onto the mattress, she threw an arm around her. "No idea. But holy shitballs, we had fun. You should have stayed."

A prim throat clearing had Kat rolling her eyes as she

glanced over at their other roommate, Maureen Park, who was sitting on the edge of her single bed.

Maureen was in her fifties and single, and Kat took secret delight in knowing she'd stolen her gnome from her front garden, and he was now happily residing on Chloe's back deck.

"Ladies shouldn't curse." Maureen's mouth pursed unattractively and Kat forced herself to bite back a comment about feline assholes.

"First, fuck you," Kat said. "And second, I'm not a lady. In fact, none of us are. You know how I know that? Ladies do not smell like we all do. Ladies definitely shower more than once a week, which is all we're allocated thanks to Jim-bloody-Boston."

"Jim Boston is the only thing holding Sanford together right now," Maureen replied haughtily, pulling on her shoes and opening the door to their shared room above The Strumpet. "And you'd do well to remember that."

The door slammed behind her.

"Someone woke up on the wrong side of the bed." Kat shrugged at Chloe.

"Kat..." Chloe sighed, slumping back against her pillow. "You need to... tone it down a little, okay? Everyone's struggling at the moment."

The smudges under her friend's sunken eyes seemed even darker than the day before, and Kat's stomach tightened with remorse.

Two months ago, the world's population was decimated with the outbreak of Sy-V—the Syrian Virus. The United States military had bombed whole cities in an effort to contain the situation, telecommunications had ceased, and the population of Sanford—their hometown—dropped from a few thousand to less than two hundred.

In just days, society had fallen.

Sanford had become a ticking time bomb with misogynist assholes running the show, and it was only after Kat and her friends had staged a coup and taken control that things had improved for the townspeople.

That was a month ago. A month in which Jim Boston had taken it upon himself to run their community, charming everyone with his 'good old boy' persona.

Kat knew better.

Not that anyone would believe her. She was the chaotic, spontaneous extrovert who made turning up late an art form.

Sometimes even her very best friends didn't take her seriously.

Resolutely, she pushed the oily hopelessness back into the pit of her stomach. It was a practiced reaction, and something she'd managed for years. However, the current state of her life was giving the oiliness cause to thrive. It was getting harder and harder to drive down and ignore.

Guilt at her own self-pity washed over her, hot and prickly, and she swallowed.

"I'm sorry, Chlo. I know things are hard. Are you still feeling off?"

"I don't feel sick anymore. I'm just really tired, even when I've had a full night of sleep." Chloe sighed, and Kat picked up her thin hand.

"You're not eating enough."

"No one is eating enough," Chloe replied.

"Jim has to do more than ration our food." Kat got off the bed and began pacing. "We're going to starve before the end of winter if he doesn't authorize groups to go scavenging!"

"Kat..."

"No! Don't 'Kat' me. You know I'm right. Rach is his second-in-command, and I can't believe she hasn't said something already." She bit her tongue.

She was genuinely happy for Rachel that she'd worked things out with James, but they were spending so much time behind closed doors that Rachel had lost focus of how precarious Sanford actually was at the moment.

And with Chloe deep in mourning for her lost husband, and Mackenzie—their other ride-or-die platonic soulmate—still in the honeymoon phase of her relationship with Jake, Kat was... something. Her throat thickened with the promise of tears.

"I hate that we have to room with Maureen," she pouted. "I wish it were Mac or Rachel. Or better yet, both. I don't even mind that Mac comes with Dex, and that dog stinks."

"God no!" Chloe tossed a pillow at Kat. "Then I'd have to listen to Mac have sex with my brother." She gave an exaggerated shudder. "And Rachel and James haven't learned to keep it down. They're worse now than when we were teenagers."

"Noise-cancelling headphones and Spotify are high on the list of things I miss about life before."

"I miss..." Chloe paused to think and Kat froze, cautious her friend would slip into another crying jag. Ash, her husband, had been out of town on business when the Sy-V outbreak hit, and Chloe hadn't heard from him since.

"... clean hair. And putting on makeup. You used to get us the most amazing beauty samples to play with." Chloe's wistful tone brought back the lump in Kat's throat.

"Yeah, I miss YouTube. And the product perks."

"What about the money?"

Kat threw the pillow back at Chloe.

"What would I do with money now? And you know I didn't keep any of it."

"I forgot you were always broke." Chloe grinned and some of the worry eased from Kat.

"I miss having my own supply of sanitary products, and not having to ask whoever's in charge of the storeroom for tampons." Kat picked up her puffer jacket and shrugged it on. "Do you need anything while I'm there?"

She was met with silence.

"Chlo?"

She turned back to face the bed and her stomach dropped.

Chloe's face was blanched white.

"What's wrong?"

Chloe shook her head, wordless.

"Chloe, you're scaring me." In seconds, Kat was back on the bed, dragging Chloe into an embrace. Something was very wrong.

"I think I'm, maybe… pregnant?"

"You're what?" Kat was afraid to have heard incorrectly.

Chloe and Ash had been trying unsuccessfully to have a baby for close to two years. What were the chances that *now*, in the middle of the end of the world and with a missing husband, Chloe would be pregnant?

"I haven't had my period since this all started, and I guess I just thought it was stress. But I've been nauseous and tired, and my breasts have been sore…"

"You didn't tell me your boobs were sore."

"I don't tell you everything." Chloe rolled her eyes, a tremulous smile ghosting her lips. "I can't believe I didn't realize sooner."

Ignoring the cautious fear warning not to get their hopes

up, Kat squealed and hugged Chloe closer. "You're having a *baby!*"

Buoyant elation bubbled within her, allowing her to forget, for just a moment.

THE ISSUE with getting Chloe a pregnancy test from the storeroom wasn't that Kat was afraid someone would assume it was for her. No, it had to do with her lack of credits.

She'd been hoping whoever was on duty would take pity on her and just give her the damn tampons because, come on, they were a *necessity*. It was kind of outrageous they weren't already a part of their monthly rations.

The problem was, she'd put a bottle of whiskey on her tab for the shenanigans last night. Not a good look for someone asking for a pregnancy test.

And today was not a good day for loitering outside the old Benson warehouse, which had been requisitioned into the community's supply center. Winter in Sanford was brutal at the best of times, and these were not the best of times.

A lack of food rations meant it didn't matter how many layers she put on. The wind whipped straight through her. And the drifts of unshoveled snow meant her jeans were wet from the tops of her boots to the tops of her knees.

She shivered.

"Kat."

The deep voice made her jump, the growly timbre shooting heat straight to her lady parts.

Jesus, when had Quinn Brent started to make her feel like that?

Talk about awkward. He was Chloe's cousin and, well,

Quinn. A quiet, bearded giant who liked things ordered and neat.

In other words, the exact opposite of Kat.

"Holy shitballs, Quinn. Don't sneak up on people like that!"

"You look like you're doing something you shouldn't be." He crossed his massively muscled arms across his chest, distracting Kat.

Where did he even buy clothes big enough to fit him?

"I'm getting supplies," she replied defensively.

"Supplies are inside the warehouse." He glanced pointedly around the barren landscape and then raised an eyebrow at her.

And if that subtle move wasn't the sexiest thing she'd seen, Kat would eat her hat.

If she had a hat.

"I was... investigating."

"Investigating?"

There went that eyebrow again. Kat swallowed.

"Scoping. Checking things out."

"Something I should know?" His hand reflexively touched the handgun that was attached to his belt.

"No! No, nothing like that. Just seeing who was on duty in the supply store."

"And that's important, why?" He stepped closer, crowding her back against the wall of the warehouse. "What are you up to, Kat Tenor?"

"I need to extend my credit a little," she admitted. "And I was seeing how favorably that request would be considered. If Maureen or Caroline are on, I'm shit out of luck. But if it's Jesse or Tabitha, I have a chance." She shrugged her shoulders in what she hoped was an innocent fashion.

"If you need something, Kat, you ask me," he stated, his eyes blazing. "I've told you that."

Yeah, he had. And Kat had immediately dismissed it. She didn't need her best friend's older cousin thinking he had an obligation to look after her.

"Seriously, it's not a big deal. I'm working in the greenhouse today and I'll get the credits to pay it back this afternoon."

He didn't look appeased, but he stepped back a little. "Jesse's on. He'll help you out."

Kat grinned. Jesse was cool. Also, she suspected he had a thing for Chloe, which Kat was still deciding what she thought of. Clearly, he had exceptional taste in women. And she desperately wanted her friend to be happy; with Ash gone, Jesse could bring Chloe out of her darkness. Make her happy again.

Maybe.

"I'm on guard duty with Tony Mitchell. Come get me if you need me."

"Sure, Q. Have a great day in this glorious weather." She winked at him over her shoulder as she headed into the warehouse.

As much of an evil, misogynistic bastard as Mayor Townsend had been, he'd had the foresight to set up the Sanford community with an exceptional system of storing and re-distributing the supplies necessary to keep them all alive.

The Benson warehouse was catalogued and ordered, with every square inch utilized. Jesse was standing behind an enormous counter, which had been taken from the local hardware store. He looked up as Kat approached.

"Uh uh, Kat. I have a note here from Caroline that you've maxed out your credits." He shook his head at her, smiling. "And don't even try to sweet talk me. Caroline will have my balls."

"Pfft. Caroline won't do shit."

"You know if you just turned up to the jobs you were scheduled for, you'd have enough credits for anything you wanted," Jesses suggested, unhelpfully.

"I have more important things to do than keeping to Jim Boston's schedule." She turned her back to the counter and hoisted her ass up and onto it, before spinning around and hanging her legs over the back so she was facing an amused Jesse.

"Besides, it's not about what I *want*, it's about what I need. You're not going to deny me necessities, are you?" She batted her eyelids.

"Like that bottle of whiskey you put on your account yesterday?"

"It was medicinal." She smirked. "I just need some tampons, okay?"

And a pregnancy test.

He rolled his eyes and gave a mock sigh. "They're on the house."

Slipping from the counter, Kat punched him playfully on his arm as she headed to the pharmacy aisles. "Thanks, Jesse!"

———

KNOCKING SNOW FROM HIS BOOTS, Quinn entered the whiskey distillery attached to The Strumpet. The corner of his mouth tipped up, remembered Kat's comment about the *glorious* weather.

Although only mid-afternoon, it was already darkening outside–another snow storm on its way. Not exactly glorious. A fresh dump on their already snow-laden surrounds was going to make moving around outside almost impossible.

But if they'd learnt anything since the world had fallen, it was to stay on their guard.

Their perimeters still needed to be defended, no matter the conditions.

They had turned the atrium foyer of the Distillery into the community's main hub and even this early, people were already coming in for their evening meal.

He waved at Jake and Mackenzie and made his way over to Jim Boston, who was at the radio controls.

"Clocking off from my shift." He handed his walkie-talkie over to Jim.

"You pulled a double?" Jim asked, placing the handset on a shelf behind him.

Quinn nodded, running a hand over his beard. "Figured I was already wet and cold. May as well save someone else from getting that way." He didn't mention he wanted the extra credits to give to Kat. Guard duty earned double what any other job did.

"Nothing to report?"

"Nope. You?" Quinn tipped his chin at the ham radio Jim was manning.

"Some chatter from a group in New York City. They've had contact from people claiming they were CDC, looking for anyone who'd had Sy-V and survived."

"You think that's even a thing?"

"What? The CDC still being operational, or someone surviving Sy-V?" Jim's hand rose to his chest to tug at a coach's whistle that wasn't there anymore. Old habits die hard.

Quinn shrugged. It didn't really matter. Even if either

of those were true, it wouldn't affect their small community as they struggled to survive through the winter.

"Dad, Mom wants you to mind Archer for a bit." Stephanie, Jim's teenage daughter, came to stand beside Quinn, a toddler on her hip. She passed the kid over and then disappeared before Jim could argue.

"Babysitting duty." Quinn grinned, glad it wasn't him.

"Apparently it's not babysitting when it's your own," Jim said. But he didn't look like he minded, and Quinn was reminded that Jim and his wife Caroline had been separated from their kids for weeks when this all blew up.

"Any idea what the teens have been getting up to?" Jim asked, his eyes tracking Stephanie as she exited the Distillery. "Kat's not leading them astray, is she?"

The faint accusation in his tone immediately had Quinn's back up, and his jaw ticked in annoyance. That was the only thing he didn't like about Jim Boston, the undercurrent of animosity he had towards Kat. Quinn didn't understand it, and he'd noticed it was reciprocated by Kat. However, whatever bad blood was between them wasn't acknowledged—even Chloe didn't know what the hell it was about.

"Hey, honey. Are you off soon?" Caroline approached them, frowning when she saw Archer. "Where's Steph? She's meant to be looking after Archer. I was hoping we could have five minutes to ourselves."

Quinn took that as his cue to leave, heading over to the rows of trestle tables where Jake and Mac were sitting. Whatever they were eating smelled amazing, and he guessed Mackenzie had been on kitchen duty again. He didn't know how she made their meals taste so good with the limited ingredients she had, especially with the amount of people they were cooking for.

"Smells good." He sat beside Jake and plucked a potato from his cousin's bowl of stew. "Tastes good, too."

"Get your own," Jake growled, swatting at his hand with a fork.

At Jake's growl, Mackenzie's dog, Dex, lifted his enormous German Shepherd head and Quinn's balls shrivelled. Just a little. He'd seen that dog rip a man's throat out for threatening Mackenzie.

"Where is everyone?" Quinn glanced around, but didn't see any of the others.

Since this had started, they'd formed a group within their community, forged through the shared experience of survival. Their bond was stronger than blood.

Kat, Chloe, Rachel and Mackenzie had always been tight, but now he and Jake, James and Jesse, were just as much a part of their found family.

The eight of them tried to share a meal together every evening, and were usually joined by Cassie and Stephen—the teenagers Rachel had taken under her wing.

"Jesse was just shutting up the supplies store, and Chloe was on her way here. Not sure about Kat, but I know Rach and James were on laundry duty, so we won't be seeing them." Mackenzie smirked.

No-one minded getting laundry detail, because the several generator-run clothes dryers heated the small room into a steamy haven. And Quinn could only imagine how a couple could take advantage of the privacy and the convenience of front-loading washing machines.

His mind instantly flashed to Kat, an image of lifting her onto a washer and wrapping her legs around his waist, causing his chest to tighten.

He shifted uncomfortably.

Apocalypse or not, Kat was just as unattainable now as

she'd been since he'd first noticed her at high school. He'd always known her, of course. She and Chloe had been joined at the hip since middle school. But it wasn't until she was a freshman and he a senior that he'd *noticed* her.

She was someone you gravitated toward–her effervescent energy contagious. It didn't help that the summer before she started high school, she transformed from a pretty kid into a stunning teenager. And he wasn't the only one who'd noticed–the boys flocked to her.

Something had happened though, that year. Her light had dimmed, and she'd stopped flirting. And then she was with Tessa Hall.

Quinn had heard that Kat's mother had tried to pay her to stop being a lesbian, and Kat had laughed and taken Tessa to Homecoming.

Since then, she'd dated women and men, but according to Quinn's discrete monitoring, nothing serious. As frustrated as he was by his quiet obsession, he couldn't help himself.

Kat captivated him.

"Maggie's ropeable that Kat didn't turn up at the greenhouse today," Mackenzie continued. "Apparently Caroline's keeping tabs on Kat and she was a real bitch to Maggie when she realised Maggie had been covering for her."

"What is it with Caroline and Kat?" Jake asked.

Mackenzie just shrugged, leaning down to feed Dex a piece of meat from her stew.

"So where was Kat if she wasn't at the greenhouse?" Quinn forced his brow not to furrow. No one needed to know the depth of his fixation.

He wasn't fooling Jake, who gave him the side eye.

"Who knows? But she's pissing off a lot of people. I'm going to talk to Rach and Chloe. We need to have a chat with her." Mackenzie sighed. "And I'd really like to talk to our group about approaching Jim and seeing what his plans are to get through the rest of winter. I swear every time I'm in the pantry there's less than there should be."

Their food supplies had also been on Quinn's mind. Mayor Townsend had set them up with supplies of every other kind, but food was something they already had to ration. Jim had been resistant when Quinn had brought up the idea of scavenging trips outside of Sanford, but it was something they needed to consider, and he knew Rachel would agree.

Around them, the Distillery foyer was filling, and Jesse and Maggie joined them at their table. Giving up on waiting for Kat to arrive, Quinn went to get his own dinner.

Tabitha was serving and, seeing it was Quinn, she gave him a double serving without blinking. As guilty as Quinn felt about eating more than anyone else, he was also twice the size of anyone else and needed the sustenance.

"Thanks, Tab." He nodded at her.

A high-pitched, angry voice had him spinning around, cursing as the hot stew slopped onto his hand.

"First you poison my husband, and now you expect me to survive on this amount of food?" Peta Berryman, having just accepted a bowl, threw her dinner.

The bowl shattered on the floor, causing those around them to jump out of the way of the mess. Anxious faces turned to Jim, who strode over.

Quinn stepped back, thankful he didn't have to deal with this kind of drama.

"Peta, everyone is given the same amount." Jim scowled, looking at the stew now on the floor.

Quinn stepped back further. No need to inflame the situation with Peta seeing his own heaped bowl.

"It's not enough! At least when Townsend was alive, we were getting fed properly," Peta cried, the whiney edge to her voice grating on Quinn's nerves.

Peta wasn't the only resident causing unrest.

When Quinn and his group had deposed Townsend, they'd also had to act as judge and executioner of Townsend's cronies. Peta's husband, Todd, had been one of those killed by ingesting anti-freeze.

"Give it a rest, Peta." Rachel appeared, face flushed and flanked by James. "When Townsend was alive, you may have been getting enough to eat, but not everyone was. And let's not forget he was forcing women to be sex slaves. I hate to be the one to tell you, but your husband was happy enough to take part in those activities."

"How dare you!" Peta's already pinched face screwed up tighter and she stepped towards Rachel.

"That's enough!" Jim moved between them, his hands raised. "I understand your anger, Peta. But we've allowed you to stay in this community, on the condition you put aside your differences and work with us."

"Differences? You *killed* my husband! When everything goes back to normal, you're going to jail. Mark my words."

"This *is* the new normal," Rachel spat. "There's no going back. Only forward. Most of the world's population is gone. You can always leave. No one is forcing you to stay."

"Fuck you!" Peta sneered and marched off, Bronwyn Stewart and Mrs. White on her heels.

Tracking their exit, Quinn wondered how much those women knew of what their husbands and sons had been doing when they ruled Sanford with Townsend. Bronwyn was a piece of work, and he couldn't imagine she didn't know what had been going on.

"We need to do something about them," Rachel warned Jim, her eyes also trained on the departing women. "They're stirring up the other women, too."

All up, there were nine mothers and wives who'd lost their loved ones when Sanford had been rescued from Townsend's clutches, and Quinn knew Kat had taken it upon herself to keep an eye on them. They needed to check in with her to find out what she knew.

But first, he had to find her.

CHAPTER TWO

DAY 62

Kat had got in late the night before, when Chloe was already asleep. As usual, she'd awoken early and had been lying awake for twenty minutes, waiting for Chloe to wake up. Finally, impatience got the best of her and she rolled over noisily.

When that only elicited a soft snore from her bedmate, she stretched out her leg and knocked it against Chloe's.

"Sorry, Chlo."

Chloe startled awake at the loud apology, blinking sleepily at Kat.

"What are you doing?"

In answer, Kat pulled the blanket over both their heads to hide them from mouth-breathing Maureen. And that wasn't an exaggeration. Her breath was creating actual clouds in the freezing air.

"So?!"

"Kat, what are you *doing*?"

"If you don't tell me whether you're pregnant *right now*, I'm going to smother you with this pillow," Kat threatened.

A slow smile broke over Chloe's face. "Are you ready to be an aunt?"

Kat put a fist in her mouth to muffle her squeal.

"I can't believe you're, what? Three months pregnant? And you didn't even know!"

"We've had a bit on," Chloe replied drily. "Ash is going to lose his mind when he finds out."

The smile slipped from Kat's face. "Chlo..."

"Don't, okay?"

Kat knew she was walking a fine line, but the stakes had just amplified. Chloe's determination that Ash would come home had been worrying, because eventually she was going to have to face reality, and it wasn't going to be pretty.

Now, though, the crash might affect the health of her pregnancy.

She opened her mouth to speak, but Chloe beat her to it.

"I mean it, Kat. Ash is going to meet this baby."

"Would you two go back to sleep?" Maureen called out.

Kat popped her head out from beneath the covers and glared at Maureen's back.

The number of times she thought "fuck off" when someone was talking was getting out of hand. Even for her.

Her eyes snagged on her backpack and she remembered the gift she'd got yesterday. Levering the top half of her body out of bed, she grabbed at the bag, pulling it back onto the bed with her.

Yawning and shivering, Chloe emerged from beneath the blanket and screwed up her nose in Maureen's direction.

Kat gasped in mock outrage. "Chloe Brent-Maxwell, was that you being *bitchy*?"

"Shut up," Chloe whispered, pushing a pillow into Kat's face.

"That's not very nice." Kat pushed back, grinning. "Especially considering I have a present for Baby Peanut."

"Baby Peanut?"

"You got a better name?"

Chloe's answering smile was soft. "No. Baby Peanut is perfect."

Kat had evaded Quinn's sharp eyes on guard duty, slogged through knee-deep snow and then ripped off a fingernail jimmying open the back entrance to Esmerelda's Gift Emporium, but the effort was worth it when she presented Chloe with the cloud-soft Merino wool baby blanket she'd taken. She'd even wrapped it in the shop's signature emerald tissue paper.

"Oh! Kat, it's gorgeous." Chloe rubbed the blanket against her cheek, tears filling her eyes. "How did you get this?"

"Just something I picked up."

"Kat! Don't pretend this isn't a big deal. I'm serious. How on earth did you get to Esmerelda's?"

"I have my ways." Kat waggled her eyebrows.

They both looked up as Maureen lumbered to her feet. "You two are impossible!" she snapped, grabbing an armful of clothes and huffing out the door, presumably to the shared bathroom on their floor.

Kat dissolved into giggles at the horrified look on Chloe's face.

"She'll get over it," she assured. "You've got to stop caring what other people think."

There was a knock at the door, and then Cassie popped

her head through. The teenager was smart and resourceful, and Kat enjoyed her company. Lately, she had been spending a lot of time with the small group of teenagers, preferring their no-bullshit approach to most of the adults in their community.

"Morning, Cass," she called, gesturing for the girl to come in.

"Stephen's waiting for me. I won't stay. Just wanted to know what you needed today?"

Kat could *feel* the questions in Chloe's gaze, but she ignored her.

"Can you check in on Asaad for me? Lucy mentioned yesterday she thought he was getting more withdrawn. I'm hoping you kids might cajole him into having breakfast at the Distillery."

"Sure. I'm also going to ignore you calling us 'the kids'." Cassie rolled her eyes.

"And I'm going to ignore you rolling your eyes at me."

They heard Cassie laughing as she shut the door and moved away.

"Holy shitballs, it's freezing in here," Kat complained, regretfully leaving the warmth of the bed and shrugging into her puffer jacket.

"It's colder than usual," Chloe agreed, snuggling further under the covers. "But don't try to distract me. Why is Cassie reporting in to you? What have you got going on, Kat?"

Hunting for her gloves, Kat shrugged. "Jim isn't giving the teenagers any responsibility, and they're bored. I'm utilizing them."

"Utilizing them?" Chloe raised an eyebrow. "Should I even ask what that means?"

"Nope."

Kat sat back down on the edge of the bed, facing Chloe. "I'm heading out. But Chlo, you need to eat more. Especially now. Tell Tabitha that you're pregnant and make sure she gives you extra rations."

"I'm not ready for everyone to know yet. You have to promise you won't tell anyone."

"Tabitha can keep a secret," Kat protested.

"No. Not yet." Chloe's voice was unusually firm. "But I'll make sure I eat breakfast, promise."

Kat was gearing up to get her own way when the door burst open, startling them.

"Kat!" Cassie was red-faced and frantic, Stephen on her heels. "Asaad. He's dead."

"What?" Kat sprang up, catching at Cassie's flailing arms. "What do you mean?"

"Exactly that," Stephen replied, voice grim. "He didn't answer our knock, but the door was unlocked. When we went in..." He paused. "It looks like he froze to death. He's at the end of the corridor and it's even colder down there. I don't think the heat was on at all."

"Are you sure he's... dead? And not in, like, a hypothermic state where he's barely breathing?" Kat knew she was clutching at straws. Cassie and Stephen weren't stupid; if they said Asaad was dead, then he was.

"The heat was out?" Chloe asked, disbelievingly. "How could that happen?"

"Jim-fucking-Boston," Kat spat. "He's managing the generators and our fuel. He won't let anyone else even *look* at them."

"What do we do?" Cassie asked.

"We get answers."

. . .

21

THE DISTILLERY'S atrium turned the foyer into a virtual ice-box. It was insanely cold and the gathering crowd had already fogged up the windows to the outside world, their breaths crystalizing as they expelled it.

They were milling anxiously, aware of Asaad's death and exhausted by the constant battle to stay alive in this new world.

They were weary.

Chloe, as Sanford High's guidance counselor, had already expressed concern about the mental load the community was collectively carrying. The dead had been buried, but they lingered. There was a pervading PTSD that was causing depression and anger. Anger that hadn't had a tangible target. Until now.

James pushed through the crowd to find Kat, sadness etched across his brow. He was the one who had first met Asaad and Lucy, and then brought them to Sanford.

"I'm so sorry, James," Kat said when he reached her side.

"This is bullshit. We're meant to be safe now, re-building. And then one of our own freezes to death in his own bed." James' lips flattened, his frustration clear.

At that moment Jim and Caroline entered the Distillery, the crowd parting to let them approach the tasting bar, which had become the unofficial front stage.

"Why is the heat off?"

"Our kids are going to freeze!"

"What happened to the generators?"

Jim raised his hands, acknowledging the questions. The crowd quietened.

"I'm sorry. I'm so sorry this happened." Jim paused, as though struggling for words, and Caroline put her hand on his arm. Ever the supportive wife.

"It appears someone siphoned gas from the generator heating The Strumpet." He was met by horrified silence.

"Who would do that?" Chloe called out.

"Blaming someone for taking the fuel is convenient, when you're the one in charge of running the generators," Kat added, raising her voice to be heard above the muttered rumblings around her. Her heart was thumping madly in her chest, and she knew she was risking what little credibility she still held by speaking against Jim. She wiped clammy palms against the leg of her jeans. "Maybe you forgot to re-fill the generator?"

"I didn't," Jim stated firmly.

The people around Kat were nodding their heads, as though they'd all personally seen Jim tend to the generators that kept them alive.

"Okay," Kat conceded. "But maybe now is a good time to question whether you should be the only one in charge of our fuel reserves and the management of the generators."

"Someone *stole* the gas!" Caroline cried. "That's what we need to be focusing on."

This time it was Jim putting a hand on Caroline's arm, a silent reproach for her lack of composure.

"You're calling one of us a thief?" Maggie called out.

"Why would we jeopardize our own safety like that?" Jesse asked. Kat hadn't realized he had joined them, his body angled protectively against Chloe.

No one here would be stupid enough to do that. Or have a reason to.

Kat was convinced that Jim's negligence had caused this. He just didn't want to admit it.

"We need to ask whether you're the right person to be leading us," she said, voice raised to be heard.

"Kat, no," Chloe warned softly.

"Are you putting up your hand?" Jim's voice was dripping in condescension.

"You can't even manage yourself, let alone a community," Caroline agreed.

"Not me. But when we got rid of Townsend, we agreed to create a board of townsfolk who would govern, and set up an election process to appoint a leader. That hasn't happened."

"Now isn't the time, Kat," Rachel called out, coming to stand beside Jim at the bar.

With a flushed face, Kat stared mutely at Rachel.

The embarrassment of her best friend publicly siding against her was bitter.

What was Rachel doing?

"Right now, we need to band together. There's no point in allocating blame," Rachel continued. "We have to work out what happened and make sure it doesn't happen again."

"But someone *is* to blame!" Kat argued hotly, hating that it was Rachel she was challenging.

Rachel glared at her, and the oily feeling inside Kat roiled, pushing its insidious tendrils out to band her chest, making it impossible to draw a proper breath.

"You wouldn't be defending him if it was a child who had died. We have vulnerable people in our community who need us to do the right thing!" Kat felt Chloe stiffen beside her, but she couldn't stop. She needed Rachel to understand what was at stake. "What if it was Chloe?"

"Chloe?" Rachel drew her eyebrows down in confusion.

"Kat, don't!" Chloe grabbed at Kat's forearm.

"She's pregnant. Are you going to risk her and her unborn baby?"

As soon as the words left her mouth, Kat wished she

could stuff them back inside. A hollow pit bloomed in her stomach as the room stilled, unbearably silent.

"What?" Rachel, face white with shock, darted her gaze between Kat and Chloe.

With an anguished sob, Chloe turned from Kat and pushed her way through the crowd and away.

Kat bowed her head, wishing the floor would open up and swallow her. What had she just done?

———

WELL, shit. Quinn made his way through the Distillery as the crowd digested the news of Chloe's pregnancy, catching Kat's arm as she spun around to go after Chloe.

"She's going to need time," he said softly into her ear. "Leave her."

"No! I can't leave her. This is all my fault."

The anguish in Kat's eyes had his heart twisting. He knew she already regretted her impulsiveness. It was what Kat did–act first and ask forgiveness later.

He didn't hold it against her. There wasn't a mean bone in Kat's body and wishing you could change her was like wishing you could catch the wind.

"I'll go." It was Jesse, his face carefully blank. Quinn wondered how the news would affect him–it was obvious he had a thing for Chloe.

"She hasn't eaten yet this morning..." Kat didn't lift her head to look at Jesse. "Will you take her breakfast, please?"

Jesse nodded and left.

With the advantage of his height, Quinn saw Mac and Jake, with Dex on their heels, also hurrying after Chloe. She would be fine.

Kat, though? She would take this badly.

"Hey. Hey." He put a finger under her chin to tip her face to his. "It's going to be okay." A single tear slipped down her cheek. Cupping her face, he wiped it away with his thumb, his chest aching for her.

"Okay, everyone," Jim called out. "Listen up."

Quinn dropped his hand as Kat turned to face the front.

"We will get to the bottom of this, but in the meantime, our priority needs to be getting the generators back up and running. We should also do more to insulate the rooms at The Strumpet," Jim continued.

Rachel nodded, looking thoughtful. "When Townsend made us strip the houses in the Evac Area, we rolled up carpets and floor rugs," she said. "I think they're stored at the back of the warehouse. We could line the floors and walls of the rooms with them."

Kat was shaking her head, jaw tight. "Get to the bottom of what?" she muttered. "That he endangered us all by not managing the generators?"

Standing behind her, Quinn ducked his head to speak into her ear, his chest pressing against her back. "I don't know what's between you and Jim, but this isn't the hill to die on. I saw Jim filling up the generator yesterday–it wasn't his fault."

Kat's whole body stilled. Slowly, she turned her head to look at him, biting on her full lower lip.

Quinn cursed himself. Now wasn't the time to be imagining those lips wrapped around his dick.

Hell, who was he kidding? He didn't need to have her in front of him to be thinking what it would be like to be with her; it was a near-constant loop in his brain. Had been for years.

"We've got a problem."

All eyes swung to the Distillery entrance, where Chris

Denning was standing, flanked by Matt Drew and Gunner Robbins. All men who'd been a part of Townsend's crew, but deemed worthy of receiving the antidote to the poison that was used to take Townsend and his cronies down.

"Quit with the drama, Chris. What's happening?" Rachel snapped.

As one, the crowd looked at Rachel, and then back to Chris.

It would have been funny, but Quinn knew in his gut this was anything but.

"Tabitha and Jean are in the pantry, taking stock. But," Chris paused, and Quinn didn't think it was for effect. Whatever the man had to say, it wasn't good. "The food's gone. Most of it, anyway. Someone raided the storeroom and kitchen last night."

The simmering energy of the room exploded.

Kat actually cowered back against his chest in response to the instant decibel rise of noise in the space. People were yelling questions at both Chris and Jim, and several were loudly wailing.

Instinctively, Quinn threw an arm around Kat, anchoring her to him amid the chaos that had erupted.

"Settle down!" Jim boomed. Although he'd raised his voice, he projected calm authority. As the room quieted, he held up his arms in a placating gesture. "We will sort this out. Panic won't help anyone."

Chris, Matt and Gunner had made their way to stand beside Jim, faces grim.

"That isn't the worst of it," Chris said.

"What's worse than no food?" Caroline asked. She blanched at the sharp glare her husband sent her, clamping her lips together.

Quinn could imagine a lot of things worse than no food,

27

and he had the sudden urge to pick Kat up and get the hell out of there.

"The fuel tank is gone."

The sudden silence was suffocating.

No fuel meant no heat. And in Sanford in the middle of winter? That meant death.

"What do you mean, gone?" Jim's voice wasn't so steady now.

"It looks like someone has come in with a snowplough and taken it," Chris admitted.

Quinn chewed this new information over carefully. Chris, Matt and Gunner had been on guard duty last night.

"How did someone get past you with a *snowplough* and you didn't notice?" Jim was definitely no longer calm. If it had been Townsend still in charge, the three men would have a bullet in their foreheads already.

Quinn had to fight his own impulse for violence, his fists clenching. These men had just sentenced their community to incredible hardship, if not certain death.

"Okay! Everyone!" Rachel's face had paled, but her voice was strong. "We aren't just a community. Not anymore. Sy-V has made us a family, and we're going to need to stand together now more than ever."

"Speak for yourself!" Peta called out, ever the delightful human. Kat stiffened again against Quinn, and he saw James step closer to Rachel. "You're not my family. I can look after myself." Peta, together with Bronwyn, Mrs. White and several others, pushed their way through to the exit, leaving a trail of open mouths in their wake.

"Oh, come on. That wasn't unexpected," Kat said under her breath. "Those women have been working against us this whole time."

Interesting.

Quinn needed to ask Kat later what she meant by that. If anyone knew what the sentiment was in their community, it was her. With her insatiable curiosity and vivacious nature, she easily mingled with all groups of people, an asset that wasn't acknowledged but was just as valuable as working in the hydroponic garden.

At the front, Rachel clapped her hands sharply, drawing the attention of the increasingly volatile crowd.

"Enough!" Rachel shouted, her gaze roving to connect with every individual before her. "If we don't work together, we're dead." Her stark words brought a stillness over the foyer, the shuffling of feet and the howling wind outside the only sounds.

Kat stepped away from Quinn and spoke into the silence.

"We need to get into a circle," she declared.

"Kat, not now," Rachel reprimanded, her tone exasperated.

"Yes, now." Kat began physically shifting those around them, until the crowd began to numbly follow suit, forming a circle around the edges of the room. "We're in this together, so let's act like that." Kat came to a stop before Rachel and Jim. "We don't need you talking at us. Join the circle, and let's work together to figure this out."

When everyone was reluctantly in the circle, Kat walked into the middle of it, spinning slowly. "See? Now we can all see each other, and everyone gets an equal chance to speak."

Rachel nodded begrudgingly.

"Well, this is cozy," Caroline sniped. "What do we do now?"

"We send teams out to scout for supplies." Quinn cleared his throat. He didn't enjoy the weight of eyes on him. "We can siphon gas from the snowmobiles we've been using and fill three or four of them. But we've only got an hour, maybe two, before this snow storm hits. We should consolidate the rooms at The Strumpet and insulate them, like Rachel said."

"We'll be hungry, but we'll be warm," Rachel agreed.

"The storm shouldn't last long." Jim's voice was louder than it needed to be. "And then we'll send out teams. The priority should be insulating the rooms. Chris, Matt and Gunner, you start moving the rolls of carpet over from the warehouse. James, find Jake and Jesse and get as many hammers and nails as you can—"

"Hold up." Quinn pointed around him. "We're in a circle for a reason. Does anyone have anything to say?"

At his invitation, a conversation started up, disclosing several small stores of food in people's rooms. It wouldn't be enough to stop their stomachs rumbling, but they shouldn't starve before they could get out to find more.

Movement at his periphery caught Quinn's attention, and he watched with narrowed eyes as Kat slipped from the room. What was the little minx up to now?

CHAPTER THREE

The wind was picking up, and Kat had forgotten to put a beanie on. Her hair was whipping madly around her head and the tips of her ears were burning with the cold.

She would not cry. She would not think about Chloe, and she *would not* think about the look of utter betrayal on her best friend's face.

She patted her jacket pocket, alarmed to realize the mini bottle of Jack was empty.

She swallowed a sob, the freezing air raw in her throat.

It would be easy for someone to track her path through the snow as she made her way down Main Street, but she was hoping everyone at the Distillery was too preoccupied with the current crisis.

She had her own crisis to deal with.

When Stephanie had come to her a week ago, Kat's first instinct had been to turn to Rachel for help. But she already knew what Rachel's response would be.

So, together with Cassie and Stephen, she'd set up a hideaway for Steph at Nan's Antique Store. Here, Steph had hidden her boyfriend, Jez, and his little sister, Amber.

He was from a neighboring town and he and Steph had been in a secret relationship via social media for the better part of a year. When he and Amber were orphaned by Sy-V, they'd made their way to Sanford, looking for Steph.

With supplies already dangerously low, months ago the community had taken the hardline and decided they wouldn't take in strangers–regardless of circumstance. The only reason Rachel had been allowed to bring James, Asaad and Lucy in was because they'd come with a ridiculous amount of food from a commercial bakery they'd raided.

Jez and Amber didn't have anything but the clothes on their backs.

The fact the community had lost all the flour and sugar that James had brought, because of some stupid water leak that had compromised more than half their dry good supplies, meant Sanford would be even less likely to take in more mouths to feed.

Jez had proved adept at hunting, bringing in small game to supplement the meagre rations that Stephanie could share. But with the situation that was unfolding, Kat knew it was time to come clean on their fugitives.

Navigating around a heap of snow beside a street lamp– which could have been trash or could have been a small car–Kat stepped under the awning of the antique store and knocked sharply three times on the closed glass door.

Sticking her gloved hands under her armpits she stamped the snow from her boots, shivering. Holy shitballs it was cold, and those low clouds coming in promised a snow storm sooner than Quinn had thought it would arrive.

When her knock went unanswered, she huffed. Reluctantly taking off a glove, she used her knuckles to rap hard again.

Not expecting the door to be unlocked after drilling into

the kids the need for security, she tried the door handle, her stomach sinking when it turned.

Stepping inside and securing the door, she looked around cautiously.

"Steph?"

The front of the shop looked like it always did, crammed with heavy antique furniture and dust-covered bric-a-brac that dated back more years than Kat cared to count. They had been careful to leave everything untouched, so the casual observer wouldn't realize the building was being used.

"Steph? Jez?" She walked further into the dimly lit space, skirting an intricately carved table topped with a pile of fusty embroidered cushions. Her nose itched and she sniffed back a sneeze.

The silence slithered forebodingly down her spine.

Where were they?

"Kat?" Cassie appeared in the doorway to the back room of the shop, her voice steeped in unshed tears. "Thank god you're here," she cried. "I didn't know what to do."

"What's happened?" Kat rushed to take the teenager into her arms. "Where are Jez and Amber?"

"They're gone. And Steph went with them." Cassie burrowed further into Kat's embrace. "I tried to stop them, but they wouldn't listen."

"Gone where?" Kat pulled back to hold Cassie at arm's length. "Where could they go? And why? I don't understand."

"I don't think they're really orphans. I mean, they might have lost their parents, but they're not alone. I heard Amber telling Jez she wanted to go back to their group, and Jez said he was waiting for the go-ahead." Cassie shrugged. "When I asked them what that meant, Steph told me to mind my own business. She knew what was going on, or at least, what Jez wanted her to know."

"So, they've gone back to their group?"

Jim and Caroline were going to *flip* when they realized their daughter had run off with her boyfriend. A boyfriend they knew nothing about.

"That's not the worst part," Cassie whispered, her eyes filling with tears. "Stephen and I came here when everyone went to the Distillery, and caught them about to leave. They'd taken one of the snowmobiles and when we tried to stop them they said we should go with them, that Sanford wasn't going to last much longer with no fuel or food."

"*They* took the supplies from the storeroom and the fuel?"

Kat felt sick. She'd been responsible for these kids.

"Not them, they let in some people from their group last night."

"Where is Stephen?" Kat suddenly realized he wasn't here.

"He wanted to check they were telling the truth, before we told anyone what had happened. And then he was going to find you or Quinn."

"Do you know where Jez and Steph were going? Where their group is based?"

Mind racing, Kat spun and stared out the shopfront windows. They should be able to see the snowmobile's tracks in the snow, but with the impending storm, they wouldn't have long to follow them.

A flurry of snowflakes hit the glass and the wind pushed against the door, causing the bell above it to jangle ominously.

Kat snapped herself back to the present. "We need to get back and alert a search party."

"Steph's Dad is going to kill us." Cassie took a step back. "Jez didn't just take all our supplies, he took Steph, too."

"Didn't Steph go willingly?"

Oh good Lord, please *let her have gone willingly.*

It was one thing to be responsible for a teenager following her heart, but another altogether to be responsible for her being kidnapped.

"Yeah. She thinks she's in love with him."

"You don't think so?"

"Maybe. I mean, I guess?"

"Well, we don't have time to debate it. Let's go," Kat said, wrapping an arm around Cassie's waist. "And don't worry about Jim Boston. Leave him to me."

FOR THE ENTIRE time they'd been hiding Jez and Amber, Kat had craftily dodged the guards who patrolled every time she'd headed down main street.

Now, when she desperately wanted to see a patrol so she could use their radio to call ahead, there were none in sight. Not that they could see much—already the falling snow was decreasing visibility enough that they were stumbling more than walking.

"Maybe we should have waited until after the storm?" Cassie's teeth were chattering so much it was hard to understand what she was saying.

"We can't wait," Kat replied.

"We can't *see*." Cassie caught at Kat's arm as she slipped.

The oiliness sloshed in the pit of Kat's stomach, reminding her that she never made the right decision.

Should they have waited?

She tamped down on the hopelessness that threatened to overwhelm her. She would fix this. She would.

"Let's turn right at the Dairy Queen. There's almost always someone on Maple Street with a snowmobile." Kat yanked at Cassie, dragging her along.

Their boots sank into the snow, making each step forward a mammoth effort. Kat was secretly glad Quinn had been working on her personal fitness. Not that she'd ever tell him that. They slogged through the snow-covered sidewalk, trailing their hands along the shopfront buildings to orientate themselves.

The falling snow muted sound—her huffing breaths was all Kat could hear. Suddenly scared, she turned to Cassie.

"Are you okay?" Her voice was over-loud, and Cassie startled.

"This is scary." Cassie's eyes were wide. "We can't see anything."

"The Dairy Queen is just ahead."

"Maybe we should go back to the antique store?"

"We're so close." Kat winced, the inside of her nose raw from breathing the freezing air. "There'll be someone on a snowmobile and we can get a lift back to The Strumpet."

They trudged forward, the snow falling thicker.

It was cold. *So* cold.

Relief flared when Kat's hand finally brushed the corner of the building and she grinned, instantly regretting it when the cold hit her teeth.

Rounding the Dairy Queen they moved forward faster, calling out into the snowy blankness.

There was no answering call.

"We need to be louder, noise isn't travelling." Kat cupped her hands around her mouth to yell again, her throat stinging from the effort.

Cassie touched her arm and said something, but Kat couldn't hear her over the rising wind. The snow was no longer falling softly—it whipped across her cheeks.

"What if no one is here?" Cassie repeated, shouting.

Kat grabbed her in a hug, bringing her mouth to her ear. "It's just snow. We can't get lost in Sanford. We'll just have to walk back."

She tried to sound reassuring. She was the adult and it was her responsibility to get them out of this mess. But god*damn* she was so sick of her life being messy.

The need to numb herself with alcohol was ever-present.

Miserably, they began trudging onwards. Time lost meaning. They continued to put one foot in front of the other, thighs and calves aching with the effort.

What was a storm had become a blizzard and, without a beanie, Kat was losing body heat. Fast. Her face and ears were no longer burning from the cold, but were completely numb. Disorientated, she squinted through the howling wind and blowing snow. She wasn't sure which way was up, down or sideways.

This was bad. Really bad.

Cassie's hand slipped from hers, the teenager dropping behind.

In seconds she was lost from sight in the total whiteout. Frantic, Kat stumbled back, knocking into Cassie in her panic.

"What's wrong?"

"I'm too tired," Cassie said through blue lips. "Can't we just rest?"

Kat knew they should be right across the street from a row of town houses. They could break in and take shelter. But there wouldn't be anything to warm them. They were past the point of just needing dry clothes–they needed heat, or they were in very real danger of succumbing to hypothermia.

Surely they weren't too far from the distillery?

"It's not much further. Come on, Cass. You can do it."

Lethargy was setting in for Kat, too, but she refused to give in. They were getting back to safety, damn it.

"I can't. I can't go any further." Cassie shook her head adamantly.

Kat grabbed the teenager's upper arms. "You can*not* give up. You give up now, and we're dead. Not just you, but me, too. Because I'm not leaving you alone out here. So get your big girl pants on and let's get moving."

Still, Cassie didn't budge, her shoulders slumped in defeat.

True terror sliced through Kat. If she couldn't get Cassie to keep going, she'd have to find them shelter. But how in hell was she going to warm them both? What use was shelter if they still froze to death?

Something bumped against her lower legs, causing her to stumble sideways. A low 'whuff' making her realize it was Mackenzie's dog, Dex. He nosed into the hand she stretched out and sweet relief coursed through her veins, warming her from the inside out.

"Dex! Good boy. Who's a good boy?" She crouched in the snow, falling forward in a snow drift as she hugged the huge German Shepherd.

He tugged her free of the snow and subjected himself to her fawning, before whuffing again and taking a step backward, his head swinging behind him and then back to her.

Standing, Kat threw her arms around Cassie. "Dex has saved us!"

Cassie managed a weak smile and they both looked to

Dex, who whined at them before turning and trotting forward.

Instantly, he was obscured from sight.

"Shit! Dex! Wait for us," Kat cried, pulling Cassie after him.

The dog reappeared, and Kat could have sworn he sighed.

This time, he came to walk beside Kat and she marveled at the kind and clever animal. The oppressive whiteness and cruel wind was somehow manageable with Dex beside them, leaning on her leg when he wanted them to change direction. Kat put her trust in the dog and forgot about navigating, concentrating solely on forcing her body to continue onwards.

Through the cold. Through the snow. And home.

———

MANIC ENERGY RAN through Quinn's blood as he paced the front bar of The Strumpet. His fists clenched and unclenched in time to the thud of his heartbeat and his jaw ached from clenching his teeth.

Where was *she?*

It had been hours since the blizzard had set in, and in that time they'd consolidated and insulated the rooms. Now, most of the community had abandoned the distillery and sat scattered around the bar, eating their rationed food and waiting out the storm.

Quinn didn't have the patience to strategize with Jim and the others over what their next move was.

All he could think of was Kat.

She hadn't been seen her since she'd slipped out of the

meeting and Quinn's frustration at everyone's indifference was at boiling point.

"Has anyone seen Dex?" Mackenzie called out, walking over to where Chloe and Jesse were sitting at a corner booth. "I let him out for a toilet break, and he didn't come back."

Quinn's head snapped towards her. "Seriously?" His palpable anger had the three looking at him in alarm. "Kat has been missing for *hours*, and you're worried about your dog?"

"First of all, he'd not *just* a dog. And you damn well know that," Mackenzie retorted. "And second of all, Kat's doing what Kat does best. Disappearing when things get tough. She'll reappear when she's good and ready, pretending everything is fine."

"Except everything is not fine," Chloe said, eyes narrow. "I'm not sharing a room with her, just so you all know."

"Jake and I are bunking in with Rach and James." Mackenzie shrugged. "There's a spare single bed, if you can stomach sharing with your brother?"

"Done." Chloe stood up. "I'm going to get my things and move them now. What room number is it?"

"You two are unbelievable," Quinn fumed. "There is a *blizzard* out there, and you're not even slightly concerned about the safety of your best friend?"

"Cool it, man." Jesse stood too, stepping up to Quinn. Jesse wasn't a small man by any means, but at six foot five, Quinn towered over most. "Everyone's wound tight at the moment, just let it go."

Quinn bared his teeth, ready for a fight. Needing the release.

"Stop it, both of you!" Chloe angled between them and

slapped a hand on both their chests. "It's unbelievable that Kat can cause trouble even when she's not here."

"What did you just say?" Quinn growled.

But everyone's attention had swung to the front door. Frigid wind howled into the bar as Dex and two snow-covered figures stepped inside.

Stephen and Rachel had already rushed forward and enveloped Cassie before Quinn realized the other shaking person was Kat. She raised her face to look around the bar, eyes latching with his, sad and lonely.

Quinn was stalking towards his woman in a heartbeat. Because that's what she was–his woman. She just didn't know that yet.

He reached her in long strides, to find her swaying on her feet. Without a thought he scooped her up and into his arms, ignoring everyone and everything around them. Her blue lips opened in a surprised 'o' but there was no resistance in her exhausted body. She was boneless, even as violent shivering racked her.

He needed to get her warm, and fast.

Resolved, he started for the stairs that led to the rooms above. What Kat really needed was a steaming hot shower. But without the fuel for the generators, he'd have to make do.

"You don't have to carry me." She protested weakly, giving a squirm as he took the stairs fast and furious. Urgency had him in its grip and he held her tighter.

He and Jesse had claimed a tiny windowless room with a single bunkbed. The beds were ridiculously sized for Quinn's large frame, but they'd wanted to leave the bigger rooms for families and couples. They'd made quick work of laying extra carpet over the floor and used a nail gun to attach carpet to the walls and even the ceiling.

It wasn't pretty, but it would insulate them against the worst of the cold.

Reluctantly, he allowed Kat to slide down his body when he stopped to open the door, changing his mind when she faltered on her feet. Picking her up, he carried her into the room and kicked the door shut behind them.

Without the dim light from the hallway, the room was plunged into total darkness.

Kat gasped.

There was a candle and matches on the bedside table, but Quinn didn't bother with them. He needed to get Kat out of her clothes and he assumed she'd appreciate the cover of darkness.

"Quinn..."

"Shhh. Let's just get you dry and warm."

He lowered her gently, keeping her steady with his hands on her waist.

"Are you okay if I help you undress?"

"Sure." Her teeth chattered. "But I don't have any other clothes, they're– "

"You can wear mine."

That idea had a thrill of possession streaking through him, heating his blood.

Feeling her nod, he unzipped her jacket and threw it into the corner.

"I can't... can you..." She sighed. "Can you please pull off my gloves? My hands aren't working."

His heart clenched for the state she was in. Why the *hell* had she been outside in this weather?

Quickly and methodically he removed her clothing, until she stood before him in just her underwear. Her skin was icy and her shivering had turned to shaking.

"Do you trust me?" he asked gruffly.

He felt her nod again.

"I need you to say it, Kat."

"I trust you. Just hurry up with whatever you want to do, because I'm freezing."

"Get into the bottom bunk. I'm going to take my clothes off, and then get in there with you. Okay?"

She fumbled her way in the darkness, and he heard her sinking into the mound of comforters he'd heaped there.

"Hurry... up," she mumbled, digging through the piles of bedlinen.

He didn't need to be told twice. Gooseflesh broke out across his skin as he stripped to his boxer briefs. Jesus *fuck* it was cold in here.

Approaching the bed he snagged one of the blankets and tucked it beneath the mattress on the top bunk so that it fell down the side of the bottom bunk, creating a cocoon within. Holding it aside, he felt around to check where Kat was before awkwardly climbing into the bed with her.

"Make me warm," she begged.

Pulling her back against his chest he wrapped himself around her and began rubbing his hands vigorously up and down her arms.

"Ow! Stop being so rough," she complained.

"I need to get your circulation going. Stop wriggling and let me do this."

His hands felt enormous as they stroked her small body, each movement firm and sure. He didn't have First Aid training and had no idea if this was actually what he should be doing, but it felt right.

He let instinct guide him.

As the minutes bleed into each other, his rubbing turned to stroking and Kat's shaking eased until she was lying still and supple. When his movements slowed and then stopped, she mewled in protest.

"Keep going, please. Feels so good. I'm just gonna take a nap, okay?" She yawned, snuggling her ass back against his groin.

He bit back a groan.

"You could have hypothermia, for all I know," he said. "I don't think I'm meant to let you fall asleep."

"That's concussion." She yawned again.

Indecision warred within Quinn. The idea of a warm and nearly naked Kat, safely asleep in his arms, was seductive. But he honestly didn't think it was a good idea to let her sleep.

He wished he could remember what they'd done when James actually had hypothermia, but they'd had power then and had been able to warm him with an electric heater. Had Rachel let him sleep?

"Stay awake for a little bit longer, okay?" He lifted himself up and over her, so he was bracketing her small body with his. He was braced inches from her, with his elbows either side of her head and his thighs straddling hers, careful not to alert her to his fully-erect cock tucked into the waistband of his boxers.

"Talk to me." The darkness made everything so much easier.

"Um. You're on top of me?"

"I'm using body heat to keep you warm."

"Okay. It feels... nice."

"Nice?" Not exactly the adjective he'd have preferred.

"Quinn?"

"Mmmm?"

"Do you like me?"

"As a person? Or, something more?" He was sure she'd

be able to hear his pounding heart. He lowered himself infinitesimally, so his chest was brushing the tips of her breasts.

He felt her hands settle on his shoulders, pulling him down onto her further. He complied, knowing it would mean she could feel his arousal as he settled fully between her legs.

"That feels like something more." He could hear the smile in her voice.

"Kat, it's been something more for a long time," he admitted, lowering his head to the soft hair at the side of her neck. "A lot more," he murmured into her ear.

This time, he didn't think her shiver had anything to do with the temperature.

"I like you, too." She raised her hips, pressing into his hardness.

This time, he couldn't hold back his groan.

They stayed that way, breathing into the complete darkness, still and silent. Quinn was hyper aware of every small detail; the rapid rise and fall of her chest, the smooth cotton sheet beneath his palms, the woodsy incense scent to the carpeting that permeated the room.

Her hands fell from his shoulders, and she sighed.

"But do you think I'm a good person?" Her voice was a whisper, but he heard the uncertainty and he swallowed against the ache in his throat.

Lowering his head to her temple, he brushed his lips against the tell-tale wetness of tears. "Kat, darlin'. You have the biggest heart of anyone I know."

She hiccoughed, and then her hands were back on his shoulders, fingers kneading.

"Quinn, will you kiss me?"

CHAPTER FOUR

Kat wished she could swallow back her words. What was she thinking? Kissing Quinn was a terrible idea.

She'd suspected for a while that he had feelings for her, which was exactly why she'd ignored the situation. She didn't do feelings. Not the emotional kind.

Once burned, twice shy, and all that.

The physical kind? Kat was *all* about those feelings. But that was as far as it went. Which was why this, right here, was so dangerous.

Quinn had no idea what he was dealing with.

His hesitation after her plea had her back-tracking. God, she was an idiot.

"Sorry. Forget I said that." The darkness, which had seemed so intimate, now hid her fake smile. She cleared her throat. "Can you–"

"Yes, I can."

And then the softness of his beard was brushing her chin and his lips were claiming hers and the exquisite tenderness had her coming undone. Just, melting.

His movements were slow and sure, his lips tasting, his

tongue exploring. She welcomed his warm intrusion, reveling in the way he was cradling her head and worshiping her mouth. There was nothing else outside this moment, outside the burn of desire that was consuming her—body and soul.

He pulled back to ghost his lips over hers. "Is this okay?"

She managed a hum of approval, tilting her pelvis. His thickly muscled thighs were spanning the outside of hers, so she couldn't widen her legs. And she was about to lose her mind if she didn't get some friction against her lady-parts.

"Words, darlin'."

"Quinn. Kiss me. And, touch me."

"Touch you?" The growly timbre of his voice was enough to make a woman spontaneously ovulate.

In answer, she tilted her hips again. "Please?"

"Darlin'," he sighed, his thumbs stroking her cheeks. "If we're doing this, we're taking it slow."

"Slow?" She blinked. She didn't do *anything* slow. She needed to wring every last drop of joy out of every experience, and then move on before someone discovered she wasn't worth their time.

She was the hype, the energy, the *party*. And she made sure to leave while the going was good, before the high ended and the taste got sour.

She would fuck Quinn, here, now, in the dark. And it would be amazing. And then she'd walk away. No harm, no foul. Leave them both wanting more.

As though reading her thoughts, he chuckled, deep and low, his beard tickling against her chin.

"I know you're not very familiar with the concept." He spoke against her lips, his mouth curved in what she could only assume was amusement. "But some things are better when they're savored."

"Nuh uh. Not true." She tried to shake her head, but he had her caged. "What if I told you I was still cold?"

"I'd call you a liar."

Her toes curled as his growliness reverberated against her. She rubbed aching nipples against his chest, certain he could feel their hard nubs.

He nipped at her bottom lip, sucking it into his mouth and letting it go with a soft pop. Damn, why was that so hot?

"I don't think you're at risk of hyperthermia anymore. But you're exhausted, sleep." He shifted his weight until he was behind her again, wrapping his arms around her. For such a big man, he was infinitely gentle.

"But—"

"No buts." He was stroking up and down her arms, deliciously soothing. "Just close your eyes. Let yourself slow down, Kat."

She wanted to protest, fight what she knew was common sense.

But, cozy and secure in the complete darkness, her eyelids drooped. He was right; she was tired. Maybe she'd just snuggle against the firm warmth of his chest and rest.

For a little bit.

THE LAST BELL *rang for the day, and Kat almost tripped over her own feet in her haste to exit the classroom. Having geometry last period on a Friday sucked balls.*

Ignoring Rachel calling out for her to wait up, she dashed down the hallway, narrowly avoiding a group of freshmen girls. Throwing her books into her locker, she grabbed her cheer uniform.

The pep rally started in half an hour and she had a precious ten minutes with him.

He barely ever text her, no matter how much she begged. The last time they'd been together, he'd said they had to stop. They couldn't keep seeing each other.

But then he'd messaged last night.

And she knew he couldn't resist her in her cheer skirt. It made his eyes go predatory and his hands greedy.

She loved it.

She had a bow in her hair and extra bounce in her step as she approached the bleachers in the empty gymnasium, and she swore her heart actually skipped a beat when she saw him.

Cheekily, she flipped her short blue and yellow skirt, thrilled at his answering growl. He tugged at the whistle around his neck, adjusting the collar of his polo.

Hugging their secret tight to her chest, she ran the last steps and threw herself into his arms.

DAY 63

KAT WOKE WITH A START, the oily slick roiling in her stomach. Struggling against the heaviness, she realized that Quinn had slung his thigh over hers in their sleep.

Out. She needed to get out.

Panic fluttered against her ribcage, and the threat of tears clogged her throat.

His soft snore told her he was still asleep. Slipping from beneath his warm bulk she rolled out of the bed, pushing at the blanket that had cocooned the lower bunk. The darkness wasn't as complete as before–she could vaguely make out the room.

It must be morning.

She had to get out of here before she collapsed in a mess of ugly crying. Her life was a shitshow, why had she complicated things further by kissing Quinn last night?

Stupid, stupid, stupid.

The icy air hit her exposed skin, and she gasped, her emotional meltdown momentarily paused as she dived for a duffle bag on the floor, riffling through until she was covered in layers of Quinn's way-too-big clothing. Belatedly, she glanced at the top bunk, remembering Quinn was sharing the room with Jesse.

Thankfully, the bed was empty. He must have slept elsewhere last night.

Rolling up the ridiculously long sleeves that hung halfway to her knees, Kat tried to jam her feet into her still-wet boots, but Quinn's socks made it impossible.

A trapped sob made her hiccough, and she stumbled.

She needed to get out.

Slipping from the room, she closed the door and leaned back against it, panting. Weak morning light filled the empty hallway and tears began sliding down her face.

Now that she was out, where was she was going to go? Chloe wouldn't welcome her back into their shared room, and it was unlikely Mac or Rachel would take pity on her. Cassie was probably mad at her and she didn't know which room Maggie was in.

Why was she such a fuckup?

She hiccoughed again.

She'd kissed Quinn, almost gotten Cassie killed in a blizzard, broken the rules and hidden outsiders. Shit. She still had to face Jim and tell him Steph was gone.

He and Caroline were probably out of their minds, worrying about where she was.

It was all too much. Just, too much.

Her knees crumpled, and she slid down the door, crouching on the freezing floor. Shoving a fist in her mouth she let the slick oiliness wash over her, drowning out the cold and any rational thought.

Teetering at the edge of the yawning pit inside her, she let go, her body racked with soundless sobs.

When the door opened behind her she squeaked, falling back against Quinn who scooped her up. Without a word, he carried her back into the room.

"Just breathe." Kissing her forehead, he locked the door and then slid his back down it until he was sitting on the floor with her still cradled in his arms.

"I'm a mess."

"I like mess."

She snuggled against him, absently noting he'd thrown on clothes before rescuing her from her meltdown. She shouldn't be taking comfort from him. He wouldn't be offering it if he knew the real her.

"You shouldn't bother with me, I'm no good at relationships."

"What if I want to?"

She fiddled with the plaited elastic hairband he always wore on his wrist.

"Do you even do relationships?" she asked. She hadn't known him to have a girlfriend.

"There's this one girl I've been waiting for."

Her stomach did a flip.

He wasn't talking about her, was he?

Hurriedly she changed the topic. "This looks like the ones I used to wear for cheerleading." She traced the yellow and blue hairband.

"It is."

"You wear a high school hairband?"

"I wear *your* high school hairband."

He... what?

"That's funny. You made it sound like I used to own it." She giggled nervously. Because that couldn't be what he meant, right?

"Kat, you're not getting it." He cupped her cheek, making her tilt her face to look at him. "This might seem fast to you, but it's been a slow burn for me. I've been dreaming about you since high school."

Butterflies erupted in her chest.

"But... you were already a senior when I was just a sophomore. How did you even know who I was?"

Quinn certainly hadn't been on her radar. She'd only had eyes for one man, and that had shattered her heart so irrevocably she'd decided she was only ever going to be with women from then on out. "And I was dating Tessa, didn't you think I was a lesbian?"

He considered her solemnly. "I thought you were bi-sexual. You are, right?"

"I feel... safer with women. But yeah, I like men, too."

"Do you feel safe with me?"

"Yes," she breathed, forcing herself not to look away from his intense gaze. "You know my mom tried to bribe me to be straight? She said she'd buy me a car if I stopped 'being ridiculous'."

"How'd that go down?"

"I bought my own car."

His laugh tunneled straight into her heart, pushing away the oiliness and making her feel lighter than she had in years. Making her feel like she could face Jim.

"If I tell you something, promise you won't get mad?"

He bent his head so his lips brushed hers, sending fireworks shooting straight to her core.

"You're too delicious to be mad at," he murmured, nuzzling down the sensitive skin of her neck. "How about we get back into bed and then you confess?"

"It's kind of something I have to do, and it's time sensitive." She *really* wished she didn't have to tell him this. The idea of spending the rest of the day wrapped in his arms beneath blankets was beyond tempting.

"I need to see Jim and Caroline."

"Okay..."

"And tell them Steph has run away," she rushed out.

Quinn stilled.

"During the blizzard?"

"Before. I'll tell you everything, but I think I better tell her parents at the same time." She screwed up her face at the thought of facing Jim.

"Kat, I don't know what it is between you and Jim." Quinn's grave expression had her stomach sinking. "I'll stand by you, but you need to sort it out with him. His daughter's life may depend on it."

———

OF ALL THE kids to have run away, it had to be Jim's.

Quinn sighed. This wasn't going to go well.

The sun was rising over a completely whitened landscape–the snow dump from the storm was the biggest they'd had so far this winter.

Maggie had gone to wake Jim and Caroline while Quinn and Kat waited in the main bar of The Strumpet. They sat side-by-side, Kat gripping his hand like her life depended on it. She was pale, and he squeezed her fingers, reassuring her.

A teenager doing a runner wasn't a great situation, but in an apocalypse? It could be a death sentence. While he wished Kat had told him sooner, he also knew that–in the blizzard–there was little anyone could have done to have chased after her.

Tabitha poured them coffee and brought it over, pretending she wasn't curious as hell about the unfolding situation. Unfortunately, there were already others awake, so this scene would not be as private as Quinn would have liked.

"No sugar, sorry hon," she said, putting a mug in front of Kat.

"Thanks, Tab." Kat released his hand and wrapped hers around the steaming mug, and Quinn felt the loss of connection.

One night with this woman, and he was done for.

Who was he kidding? He'd been done for, for years.

The temperature was already below zero, but when Jim and Caroline entered, it plummeted.

"Q. What's going on?" Jim strode straight to them, Caroline on his heels. She looked between him and Kat, zipping up her down jacket, but didn't say a word.

A pang of guilt lanced Quinn as he noticed her red-rimmed eyes and disheveled appearance. She was a mother whose child hadn't come home last night.

"Is this about Steph?" Jim finally glanced at Kat, but quickly re-directed his attention back to Quinn.

Kat's heavy exhalation before she stood created a cloud in the icy air, and Quinn's gut tightened.

"Steph has run away." Kat sucked on her bottom lip. "With her boyfriend."

Her words hung, suspended. No one spoke.

A door slammed from one of the rooms above and Quinn tensed.

"What boyfriend?" Caroline exploded, pushing past Jim to stand before Kat.

"Steph doesn't have a boyfriend," Jim countered, face thunderous.

"His name is Jez, and they'd been together for a while before the outbreak. He and his sister were orphaned, so they came to Sanford looking for Steph."

"What?" Caroline gasped, her hand flying to her mouth.

"Bullshit!" Jim spat. "My daughter doesn't keep secrets."

Kat's mouth twisted, and she looked away from Jim. "They took a snowmobile and left yesterday, before the storm. But, uh. There's something else."

Premonition prickled the back of Quinn's neck, and dread settled over him.

Kat was wringing her hands together, looking at the floor. "Jez is the one who took the fuel and food."

Oh, shit.

"What?" Jim's voice was deadly quiet. "You're telling me that a boy took my daughter and all our supplies?"

"Not just him. He had a group, which we didn't know about–"

"We?" Caroline shrieked. "How long have you known about this? Where did they go?"

Kat took a deep breath. "I don't know."

"So you don't know the *only* thing we need to know?" Jim yelled, fists clenched in frustration.

Quinn pushed back his chair, ready to stand.

"You knew about this secret boyfriend, and you didn't

think to tell us?" Caroline stepped closer to Kat. "You've always been irresponsible and careless. But this is unforgivable." There was a sharp crack as Caroline slapped Kat's cheek.

Adrenaline surged through Quinn and he leapt to his feet, stepping between the women and glowering down at Caroline.

"Don't *ever* touch her again," he growled.

"Don't speak to my wife like that." Jim pushed at Quinn's chest.

Quinn was taller, broader, younger and fitter. And he had no qualms about throwing down to protect what was his. "Stand down, Jim," he warned.

"It's okay." Kat's small hands were on his back, urging him to stand aside. Blood pounded in his ears when he turned to face her and saw the vicious red handprint on her cheek. "All that matters is making a plan to get Steph back," she continued.

"Cool your socks, Caro." Maggie pulled out a chair and gestured for Caroline to sit. Quinn hadn't even noticed Maggie come back into the room. "Tab, can you please get these two some caffeine?" she called out.

Shaking, Caroline slumped into the seat. It took a beat before Jim followed suite.

"I know it doesn't change anything, but I really am sorry," Kat said quietly.

"Girly, you need to sit, too." Maggie had always had a soft spot for Kat, and now she put her arm around her, guiding her to sit.

Studying Kat's almost-cowed stance, Quinn realized his little firecracker always lost her spark when she was around Jim. Whatever their history was, it was enough to strip Kat of her normal confidence.

He didn't like it.

Quinn lowered himself back down and the four of them sat stiffly around a small round table, conscious of the whispers around them.

"Here you go." Tabitha placed mugs before Jim and Caroline. "It's too bad coffee can't substitute for food, because we've got gallons of the stuff."

As if on cue, Kat's stomach rumbled.

Quinn wondered when she'd eaten last.

Damn! Why hadn't he fed her?

Caroline narrowed her eyes. "Looks like we can thank Kat for that."

"Back off, Caroline. Kat didn't steal our supplies," Quinn shot back.

"No, but she knows who did. Tell us about this group, and everything you know about this so-called boyfriend of Steph's," Jim demanded.

"His name is Jez, and he's the same age as Steph. I think they met at drama camp?"

Caroline sat back a little, staring into the distance. "Last summer," she murmured, as though things were falling into place in her mind.

"He turned up at Sanford a couple of weeks ago-"

"*Weeks* ago?" Jim yelled, looking like he was ready to leap from his chair and throttle Kat. Quinn slung an arm around the back of Kat's chair, silently daring Jim to mess with his girl.

"Steph came to me for help, and I couldn't turn two kids away," Kat replied defensively. "We didn't mess with the ration system. Steph shared hers when she could, and Jez hunted small game. They were staying at Nan's Antique Store and I'd told Steph she had to tell you both. She was working herself up to it."

"But now she's been taken," Jim said tightly.

"Cassie said she went willingly. She knew what she was doing." Kat tilted her chin, glaring at Jim. "I am responsible for hiding outsiders, but I'm not responsible for Steph's actions."

Quinn bent his head to Kat's ear. "Cassie knew?"

"All the teenagers did." Kat turned to him. "I swear we had no idea he was part of a larger group, or that he would do something like this. He's a nice kid."

"A nice kid who took my daughter!" Jim pushed his chair back and stood. He began pacing beside their table. "Where was he from? That should give us some idea of where they could be."

Guilt clouded Kat's features. "I didn't ask."

"You didn't ask! So you just let strangers into our community, knowing nothing about them!" Jim thundered.

"That's enough." Quinn straightened in his chair, pulling back his shoulders and drawing himself up to his full height. "*Your daughter* vouched for him. You're not laying that on Kat."

Animosity crackled in the air between them.

"What's going on?" Rachel appeared at their table with James beside her, looking between the four of them with concern. "Kat, what have you done now?" she sighed.

Quinn felt Kat slump beside him.

Oh, hell no. He was sick to death of people putting her down. And for one of her best friends to assume the worst? That was just fucked.

Quinn didn't often use his size to intimidate, but he was *done* with this bullshit.

Slowly, he rose to his full six foot five inches, standing behind Kat's chair with his arms crossed over his chest. His hard stare moved between Rachel, Jim and Caroline, daring them to say another word.

"We're all friends here, remember?" James spoke up, raising his hands in a placating gesture. "Whatever's going on, we can work it out."

"What *is* going on?" Rachel asked again.

"Jim can fill you in on the details, but for now, we need to get everyone down here," Quinn said. "We're going to need to put together two search parties–"

"We need more than two!" Caroline interrupted.

"We don't have the gas to fuel more than four snowmobiles," Quinn explained. "As it is, the groups will probably need to find more gas while they're out there, so they can get back home."

"Do you have a lead on who stole our supplies?" The hope in Rachel's voice was unmistakable.

"After Kat and I speak to the teenagers, we'll have a better idea," Quinn replied, holding up his hand when Rachel went to speak again. "Why don't you and James wake people? That way Jim doesn't waste time explaining the situation twice."

Quinn could tell it was killing Rachel not to know what was going on. She opened her mouth and closed it, finally turning away when James tugged at her arm.

ASSUMING Kat knew which room Cassie and Stephen were in, Quinn followed her up the staircase, noticing for the first time how ridiculous she looked bundled in his clothing.

She was adorable.

"Are you okay?" He slipped his hand into hers, twining their fingers together.

"It just sucks when Rach is pissed at me. It feels like

when Mom used to be all 'I'm so disappointed in you'," Kat admitted, stopping at the second floor landing.

"She's not being fair to you." Quinn's words were sharper than he'd intended.

"No, she is." Kat shrugged. "She's mad on Chloe's behalf. And also, I skipped a couple of days in the hydroponic garden and someone messed up the drip arrangement I'd installed. We lost a heap of seedlings and–"

"Kat." He pulled her body into his, backing them both into a shadowed alcove. Easily he lifted her until her legs were secured around his waist and their eyes were level. "You set up that entire garden, and it's been feeding us. It's not on you if someone else broke your system."

"But if I'd been there–"

He silenced her with a kiss, his lips slanting over hers as he showed her just how much she was worth. Her mouth parted on a breathy sigh and he took the invitation, his tongue searching, asking for more. She was deliciously drugging–like nothing he had ever tasted.

A groan rumbled in his chest as he pressed her against the wall, angling her head so he could have better access to the nirvana of her mouth. She met his hunger, dueling with his tongue and grinning against his lips when he groaned again.

"You're a brat." His hand that was holding her gave a reprimanding squeeze.

"You're meant to be telling me how wonderful I am, not insulting me." She sucked on his bottom lip, mimicking his action from last night.

His palm flexed against her perfect ass.

Voices and footsteps from the third floor had him reluctantly pulling away, depositing her back on her feet.

"Come on, brat. We've got teenagers to interrogate."

CHAPTER FIVE

Cassie had met Kat with a hug, holding no grudges for their almost-disaster yesterday. Stephen wasn't so forgiving. His glare had sharpened when he'd sniffed at the liquor on Kat's breath, and she wanted to smack him for being so judgmental.

Not that she could focus on that right now.

Not when Quinn was about to head out with one of the search and rescue missions, and she'd been told in no uncertain terms to stay put.

She looked around at the group who had gathered at the Distillery to get ready.

"Rach, can we just—"

"No. Only eight of us can go, and we've already decided who that's going to be." Rachel sighed, softening a little when she saw Kat's frustration. "I know things have been... tense. When I get back we'll talk, okay?" She pulled Kat into a hug. "You know that even when I don't agree with you, I always love you."

Tears welled in Kat's eyes and she blinked, fighting the

urge to melt into her best friend. She knew she'd stuffed up. She knew Rachel, Chloe and Mackenzie had every reason to be mad with her.

But that didn't make it hurt any less.

"I just want to help," she said against Rachel's shoulder.

Rachel pulled away and framed Kat's face with her gloved hands. "With Jim heading out, and me heading out with James, Quinn and Jesse, we need you here. You can help keep everyone reassured."

Kat didn't want to push away the olive branch Rachel was offering, but she also didn't think it was fair she wasn't being given a chance to right her wrongs. She should be going into the unknown to find supplies and bring Steph back.

"You don't even know where you're going." She pouted, stepping out of Rachel's hold. "The teenagers don't know where Jez came from."

"The *teenagers* are standing right here," Stephen said drily. "And we don't appreciate being called that."

"Stop getting triggered, Stephen." Kat rolled her eyes. "And it doesn't change the fact all you can give us is a general direction."

"*You* didn't ask him, either," Stephen responded, crossing his arms.

Cassie nudged him. "Kat spent barely any time at Nan's. We're the ones who were there all the time. And all we know is that his hometown didn't have a cinema, and he used to go to Dutton to see movies."

"Do you know where Sami is?" Kat asked her. "Can you find her, and Jimmy and Lucas, and check Nan's to see if Jez and Amber left anything behind?"

"Sure, us *teenagers* will do your bidding." Stephen grinned at Kat to show he was only stirring.

She rolled her eyes again.

"Right, we're good to roll out." Jim strode over to them, flanked by Chris, Matt and Gunner. Kat noticed his didn't look her way.

Fine, she didn't want to look at him, either.

James handed over backpacks heavy with carefully wrapped bottles of whiskey. The two teams were hoping they'd be able to use the alcohol to barter for supplies if needed.

The whiskey distillery had made Sanford a target at the beginning of the outbreak, and they weren't stupid enough to think it couldn't still put them at risk. There was a reason they'd consolidated their community into a fortified area that included the distillery, their storage warehouse, and The Strumpet.

"We've got Greenville and you're good to cover Arlington. We'll meet up at Dutton in forty-eight hours." Jim shouldered one backpack. "Let's stay in radio contact, and hope to Christ we find enough supplies to fill these trailers we're going to be towing."

It was hard to believe it was already mid-morning—the sun was staying determinedly low key and the snow-swept landscape looked bleak.

Heading outside, they watched as Jim and his group pulled away on two snowmobiles, the bitter wind whipping through Kat's layers of clothing in seconds.

She snuck her hand into Quinn's large one, and warmth rushed through her when he squeezed gently.

He bent his head to speak in her ear. "I'll be back before you know it."

She ignored a curious look from Mackenzie and a smug smile from Jake, and turned her body into the front of

Quinn, wrapping her arms as far around his waist as she could reach.

"Please be careful," she whispered, when she finally let him go.

"We've got unfinished business, darlin'. You better believe I'm coming back for that." His soft words lit her up like a Christmas tree, and she had the sudden thought Christmas couldn't be too far away.

Not that anyone was tracking a calendar these days.

Seeing Rachel get onto the back of a snowmobile with James put an ache into Kat's chest and she fumbled with the scarf around her neck, thrusting it at Quinn.

"Darlin', I've got a scarf. You need this." He tried to give it back, but she shook her head adamantly.

"Take it. Please."

When he wound it around his neck warmer and tucked the ends into the front of his jacket, she felt the ache ease some.

"Come on, Q. Let's get going," Jesse called from the other snowmobile.

Quinn brushed his thumb over Kat's bottom lip, giving her a crooked smile before walking away.

And why the *hell* did it feel like he was taking a piece of her heart with him?

Chloe stepped up beside Kat as Jesse and Quinn prepared to follow James and Rachel, hugging her mid-section and looking like she was about to breakdown.

Instinctively, Kat linked their arms, drawing her close. Chloe's slight form stiffened and then relaxed into Kat as they waved the two snowmobiles off.

They stayed standing with their arms locked, watching their disappearing friends until all they could hear was an echo of the snowmobiles. And then, nothing.

A mangy-looking dog trotted into view, running off when Mackenzie called out to it.

"You can't rescue them all," Jake said, grimacing at Mackenzie's obvious disappointment.

"I just hate the thought of all these pets with no-one to care for them." Mackenzie looked after the retreating animal, finally breaking her stare when Dex bumped his head against her leg. "I know, boy. I've got you."

"There are two or three packs of dogs getting around town, and we're going to have to deal with them soon," Stephen said. "They're hungry and vicious."

Kat shivered, remembering the pack of dogs that had been ready to attack them when they'd been escaping Townsend. She could only imagine how much more desperate the animals had become in the intervening weeks.

"Let's get back inside." Mackenzie turned away. "I want to see what exactly is left in the kitchen. We need to work out how we're going to feed everyone."

"I'll help." Chloe pulled away from Kat, but then looked back at her. "You coming?"

Swallowing her relief, Kat hurried after them back inside.

She didn't get further than the snow vestibule, because Mackenzie and Jake were blocking the door to the foyer.

"What's going on?" she asked Chloe.

"I'm not sure." Chloe touched Mackenzie's back. "What's happening?"

Suddenly, Jake and Mackenzie stormed forward, with Jake yelling something that Kat couldn't decipher.

Kat rushed after them, a current of energy sparking up her spine and her skin prickling uncomfortably.

"Stay away from her!" Mackenzie was yelling at Caroline, shoving a sobbing Cassie behind her. Cassie ran straight into Kat's arms.

"I was just–" Caroline was flustered at having been confronted.

"Back off, Caroline," Jake warned in a low growl. "I realise you're distressed about Steph, but that doesn't mean you can take it out on Cassie."

Their voices resonated off the polished concrete floor of the almost-deserted distillery, and the few people who were gathered around the ham radio were watching the scene curiously.

"Shhh, honey. It's okay." Strands of Cassie's hair were stuck to her tear-stained cheeks and Kat brushed them back. "What happened?"

"She kept saying I must know more, that I had to remember and it was my fault that Steph was gone." Cassie hiccoughed.

"Cass!" Stephen came flying across the room, Sami, Jimmy and Lucas with him. "What did you say to her?" he demanded, pulling his girlfriend from Kat's hold.

Caroline slunk away as the attention swung to Kat.

"Kat didn't say anything." Chloe defended her instantly.

Kat's legs were shaky with the intense relief that flooded her.

"It was Steph's mom," Cassie spoke up. "She wouldn't listen and kept harassing me." She choked on another sob. "She wouldn't leave me alone."

"Just stay away from her for now. I'll have a word with her," Jake said.

"Jake's right, try to keep a low profile." Kat glared at Caroline, who was now whispering with Peta on the other side of the room. "Are you guys about to head over to Nan's?"

"Yeah, I don't think they left anything, but it's worth looking," Stephen said.

"Okay. Check in with us when you get back." Kat's stomach growled, and she grimaced. "Hopefully we'll have come up with some kind of meal by then."

DEX BOUNDED around their heels as Mackenzie, Chloe and Kat walked to the distillery's employee room and kitchen, where communal meals were cooked and served.

"It's bad enough that Jez and his people stole supplies from the warehouse, but to have come in here and raided the pantry as well, that's low," Mackenzie muttered, shining her flashlight around the makeshift pantry.

The normally meticulously organised shelves were in disarray, and Kat crunched over spilled rice as she stepped inside.

"At least they didn't take everything." She began sorting through knocked over packets of instant noodles.

Dex whuffed, as though in agreement, and Kat bent to pat his head.

"I wish there were some treats here for you, Dex-boy." She looked up at Mackenzie. "He saved me and Cassie, you know. I don't think we'd have made it without him."

"I know. I love you, so he loves you," Mackenzie replied, matter-of-factly.

"Mac. Chloe, I–" Kat's apology died on her lips as Mrs. White and Bronwyn barged into the small space. Chloe stumbled into the wall to avoid them, and Kat reached out to steady her as Mackenzie threw out her arms to stop the women, who were grabbing at anything they could get their hands on.

"What are you doing?" Kat yelled, at the same time that Mackenzie bellowed at them to stop. Adrenaline shot through Kat and she felt a little dizzy.

The two women were yelling back, Dex was barking, and the enclosed area exploded into loud chaos, with reaching arms and hostile intent.

"What *the fuck* is going on in here?" Boomed Jake, arriving at the door and startling everyone still. "Get your hands off her, right now," he snarled at Bronwyn, who was pushing at Mackenzie.

"Or what? You're going to kill us, too?" Shot back Mrs. White. "Like you killed my son? And Bronwyn's husband?"

"They chose their fate when they joined forces with Townsend and turned Sanford into a misogynistic-run dictatorship." Kat refused to feel guilt for killing men who were raping women and subjugating their town to tyranny.

"We're hungry, and we're taking what's owed to us." Bronwyn turned back to the shelves and picked up a can of soup.

"That's not how this works!" Mackenzie protested. "You can't just take what you want. We have to divide it equally to feed everyone."

Mrs. White gave a brittle laugh. "Like you weren't going to be giving Chloe extra rations, now that she's pregnant?"

That *did* make Kat feel guilty, because she was absolutely going to be giving Chloe extra.

"They won't be giving anyone anything," a voice said behind Jake.

Kat's stomach dropped as Jake stepped back outside the

pantry in order to see who it was, and Kat craned her neck to see beyond him.

"Peta, what the hell?" Jake backed up, hands raised. "There's no need to point a gun at me."

Dex growled, low and threatening, and everyone in the pantry froze.

———

THE WORLD outside Sanford was quiet.

Silence wasn't something that had ever bothered Quinn, but this kind of quiet was eerie. Unsettling.

There were no vehicles on the road, planes in the sky, or people... anywhere.

None that were showing themselves, anyway.

They climbed off the snowmobiles out the front of the truck stop they'd used previously when Townsend have driven them out of town. Without the roar of the snowmobiles' two-stroke engines, the silence was deafening.

They'd been travelling for less than half an hour and Quinn was already thoroughly fucking cold. Tucking his gloved hands under his armpits he stomped over to Rachel and James.

"Why are we stopping here?" The last time they'd been here they'd taken the gas, food and anything else worth scavenging. There was nothing here but bad memories.

Something James clearly agreed with, if his tight expression was anything to go by.

"After we took back Sanford, I slipped over here and left a stash of supplies, just in case," Rachel said.

"Just in case?" Quinn knew Rachel liked to be organized, but he hadn't been aware she'd taken it this far. "Does Jim know about your 'just in case'?"

"*I* didn't know about her 'just in case'," James grumbled.

"I'll be two minutes." Rachel turned towards the door to the diner. "It's just two backpacks," she called over her shoulder.

Still grumbling, James followed her.

Jesse laughed, leaning back on their snowmobile. "Those two are the most volatile couple I've ever met." He smirked. "I'm never sleeping in a room next to them again. Have you heard how loud they are when–"

Quinn held up his hand, holding back his own smirk.

"We are *not* talking about their sex life."

"We could talk about yours then?" Jesse gave him a shit-eating grin. "Or you could thank me, for giving you your privacy last night."

"Or we could talk about my fist in your face." Quinn countered with his own grin. "Let's not... huh." He stopped, lowering his voice. "Check that out."

Not thirty feet from them, an enormous buck with majestic antlers ambled from the tree line to stand in the middle of the snow-covered highway. Slowly and without concern, the animal turned its head to face them, flaring his nostrils as he studied them.

"Would you look at that," Jesse marveled quietly. "I've never seen one so close before."

The buck showed no fear, and Quinn had the disquieting thought that in a matter of months, the wildlife were already taking back the world.

They no longer considered humans to be the dominant threat.

"Well, at least we know we can hunt to feed ourselves," Quinn said.

The buck stamped his front hoof once and then walked back the way he'd come.

Quinn remembered himself and stamped his own feet, the forgotten cold reasserted. If electricity was going to be a thing of the past, they needed to seriously consider moving somewhere warmer.

"You think they'll be okay back in Sanford?" Jesse asked, rubbing his hands together.

Quinn knew he was thinking of Chloe and, if he was honest with himself, he'd acknowledge his own thoughts rarely strayed from Kat.

"They'll stay warm, and there's enough food to keep them going." He ducked his chin so he could breathe deep against the scarf Kat had given him. Her scent of vanilla and sandalwood settled something within him he hadn't even realized was feeling ravaged.

"You're right. With the eight of us out looking for supplies, their food will stretch longer." Jesse looked Quinn straight in the eyes. "But let's not be gone longer than we need to."

They watched as Rachel and James emerged from the diner, each carrying a backpack.

"Agreed." He tipped his chin at Jesse. "Let's get this done."

THEIR DESTINATION WAS ARLINGTON, a town east of Dutton. It was smaller than Sanford, and Quinn was hopeful the lack of people would make it easier to hear or see survivors.

The decimated population had to be useful for something.

He pulled his snowmobile alongside James and Rachel and waved his arm at them to stop. They came to a standstill at a sign welcoming them to Arlington.

"We should go in on foot," Quinn called out. "These snowmobiles are too loud. If Jez and his people are here, we don't want to let them know we're coming."

James nodded, and Rachel switched off the ignition.

"How are you for gas?" James asked.

Quinn grimaced. "Low. We're not making it back to Sanford unless we find some here."

"Guys, I know there aren't many people left, but it's probably not a great idea to just leave the snowmobiles here in the open, right?" Jesse looked between them.

"I was thinking we could stash them down there." Quinn pointed to their left, at a driveway guarded by snow-laden trees. They could just make out the red roof of a small farmhouse. "Hopefully they'll have snowshoes we can use."

"Think there's anyone home?" Rachel wondered.

Quinn shrugged. "Only one way to find out."

As they made their way single-file down the narrow driveway, Quinn's shoulders tensed. It had been a long time since they'd come into contact with anyone outside Sanford, and a friendly reception wasn't something he was willing to bet on.

Sy-V hadn't just wiped out most of the world's population–it had shifted the moral compass for those left alive. Changed their perspective and regressed humanity back to the basic need for survival.

Even with whiskey to barter with, there was every chance a stranger would shoot first and ask questions never.

Jesse, riding behind Quinn, tugged on his jacket to get his attention. "Rachel's trying to tell us something."

Slowing, Quinn glanced behind them to see Rachel bringing her snowmobile to stop.

"What's wrong?" Quinn reached for the Ruger handgun beneath his jacket.

"You should let us go in front, so if there's someone there, they see me first," Rachel called, her voice creating clouds in front of her face.

Quinn hesitated. While he agreed that seeing him first might not give the best impression–folks had been cautious of his size his whole life, let alone now they were living the apocalypse–he was also very aware that women were a commodity in this new world order.

"She's right." James didn't look happy to be agreeing with his girlfriend. "If anyone's here, they'll have heard us. Best we seem as non-threatening as possible."

Reluctantly, Quinn allowed Rachel and James to pass him before following, Ruger in hand.

As the driveway widened to accommodate the front of the house, Quinn caught a flash of bright blue.

What the hell?

There was a small girl on the front verandah, bundled into a too-large jacket, grinning and waving madly at them. Jumping from foot to foot, she called out as they switched off their engines and dismounted.

"Hey! Hi! Hi there!"

Quinn wasn't great at guessing the age of children, but this little one couldn't have been older than six. Her cheeks were bright red from the cold air, and she had twin rivulets of clear snot running freely from her nose.

"Hi," Rachel called back, taking point. "What's your name?"

"Gracie. I'm Gracie, you spell it g-r-a-c-i-e. Not with a y. Who are you?" The kid wiped her sleeve across her face, smearing the snot.

"I'm Rachel, and these are my friends. Are you sick, honey?"

Quinn and Jesse shared a concerned look, and James

put his hand on Rachel's arm to stop her moving further forward.

"Nah, I don't have that vi-rus. Not the bad one. I just gotta runny nose. Mommy used to say it was daycare germs, but I haventa been to daycare in *ages*." She spread her arms wide, indicating the length of time.

"Is your mommy home?" Rachel asked.

The kid's face fell.

"Nuh uh. The vi-rus got her." She sniffed. "But my daddy is inside with my lil' brother Toby. You spell it t-o-b-y. He has a y in his name. You want me to get him?"

"Sure, honey. Can you let him know there are some friendly visitors here?"

Rachel turned to face them when Gracie ran back inside, slamming the front door.

"Think we should radio in to Jim, let him know where we are?" she asked.

"Just did it," Jesse answered, patting the radio handset clipped to his belt.

The door opened and Rachel swung back around. Quinn's hands tensed on his Ruger. A cute little girl didn't mean there was no danger.

A gangly man with ginger hair and glasses stuck his head out, the lenses instantly fogging over in the cold. Mumbling something intelligible, he took them off to wipe them and squinted at them as he stepped onto the porch.

He was unarmed and looked washed out. Tired.

"Hi," he called cautiously, pushing Gracie behind his legs. "I didn't, uh, hear you arrive."

Was he sick? Hungover? How on earth had he not heard their snowmobiles?

"We don't mean any harm, we're friendly," Rachel reassured, holding out a bottle of whiskey. Quinn wondered if giving this man alcohol was the best idea.

And then a high-pitched wail started up inside, and the man winced.

"That's Toby. I'm Mike. Do you want to come inside? It's a bit warmer."

The wailing intensified in volume as they filed inside.

"Don't worry about taking off your boots," Mike called from further down the hall. "It's too cold to not have them on."

There was a slightly funky smell, almost musky, and Quinn wrinkled his nose. The hallway opened into a living area, where a fireplace was heating the space. A cot was set up in the middle of the space, and Mike bent to pick up a screaming bundle of baby.

The crying hiccoughed to a stop and some of the tension released in Quinn's shoulders. Who knew babies could be so loud?

Mike jiggled the baby against his shoulder, the reason for his exhaustion now apparent.

"Man, we're friendly. But you probably shouldn't just invite strangers inside." Quinn didn't want to lecture, but the man appeared oblivious. "And your little girl shouldn't have been outside by herself. It's not safe."

Mike sighed, gesturing for them to take a seat on the sofas. "I know. I know. I'm just... struggling at the moment. Toby's not sleeping and..." He trailed off as Toby starting crying again.

"Here, can I take him?" Rachel didn't wait for an answer, plucking the baby from Mike's arms and rocking him as she started pacing. Miraculously, the crying stopped.

"Is it just the three of you?" James asked.

"Yeah. Liv... passed away at the beginning." Mike

rubbed at his eyes. "I didn't think there was anyone left, I thought we were alone in the world." Gracie crawled onto his lap and put her arms around his neck. "But then a week or so ago, an Army group came through town and picked it over. I'm lucky they didn't bother with the houses on the outskirts, otherwise we'd have run out of food already."

"Army?" Quinn asked, leaning forward. "What were they doing?"

"Looking for survivors. They've set up a colony or something. And, according to the one guy I spoke to, they're looking for anyone who's had Sy-V and survived. He was talking about some scientists working on a cure."

"We don't need a cure," Jesse said. "Anyone who's still alive is immune."

"This guy said something about mutations." Mike shrugged.

The baby started up again.

"He's hungry." Mike stood up and deposited Gracie back into the chair. "Can you hold him for a second while I milk Bessie?" he asked Rachel.

Milk Bessie?

As though she'd heard her name, a nanny goat–previously unnoticed–stirred from a bed of blankets beside the fire, letting out a soft bleat.

Mike laughed at their shocked expressions. "There's no formula left anywhere in town, but I remembered our neighbors had Bessie," he explained. "She smells a bit, but it's too cold for her outside, so she's an inside goat now."

With Toby still wailing, it took a moment for them to register the sound of the radio at Jesse's hip crackling to life.

"Is that Jim?" Quinn looked to Jesse, who had stood up and unclipped the handset.

"I'm not sure, the reception isn't great." Jesse brought the radio to his ear, his expression intent.

"Take it outside, see if that helps." Quinn was already standing, ready to follow him out.

The scratchy voice came over the airway again and Quinn stilled, senses suddenly on high alert. He knew that voice, intimately.

Kat's voice came again. "...forced out. We'll go... guns. ... don't come back to Sanford."

CHAPTER SIX

Kat was getting really sick of being held at gunpoint.

This apocalypse had made everyone trigger happy, and she was tired of being held hostage. Her legs were cramping from first standing, and then sitting, in the small pantry with Mackenzie, Jake, Chloe and Dex, for the last four hours.

And if she didn't get a drink soon, she was in very real danger of sobering up.

She shifted uncomfortably, straining to hear what was happening in the breakroom.

Mrs. White had just come back in, telling Bronwyn and Peta she'd sent the guards on duty to the back fence.

"We need to move them now," Bronwyn said.

Kat exchanged a look with Chloe.

Move us where?

"What's going on in here?" Kat heard Caroline ask. "We need to feed everyone, and I can't find Mackenzie."

"Caroline! I'm in here!" Mackenzie called, scrambling to her feet and accidentally stepping on Dex's tail. He yipped in annoyance.

Caroline appeared in the doorway, looking between them and the gun Peta was wielding. "I shouldn't ask, should I?" she asked, voice flat.

"Can you talk some sense into them?" Jake asked her, also getting to his feet. "This is getting ridiculous."

Kat kept her mouth shut. She didn't think Caroline would do her any favors.

"I'd advise you to walk away, and forget you saw anything," Peta suggested, raising her eyebrow at Caroline. "We know you were against the plan to poison our men, and we don't have a problem with you."

That was news to Kat. As far as she remembered, Caroline and Jim had been very much onboard with overthrowing Townsend, and all the consequences that went with it.

Not that it surprised her Jim had instigated a PR campaign to swing the people his way. If he hadn't been a football coach, he'd have made an excellent politician.

Untrustworthy, self-serving and slimy as fuck.

Kat held her breath as Caroline weighed up her options.

"Pretend I wasn't here," she finally said, turning away and disappearing from sight.

"What?" Kat's mouth hung open as she looked up at Mackenzie and Jake's shocked faces. "Did she just... leave us?"

Chloe let out a quiet sob.

Suddenly, the situation went from outrageous, to scary. Really scary.

What she'd thought was a power flex, was actually a power shift. A shift that could put her and her friends in danger.

"Get up." Peta jerked her chin at Kat and Chloe, who did as they were told.

Kat tried to ignore the pins and needles tingling through her numb foot. She had a really bad feeling about where this was heading, and the persistent thrum of longing for Quinn turned fierce.

She wanted him here, with her.

"Peta–" Kat started.

"No. Shut your mouth," Peta snapped. "You've already tried to reason and plead and persuade. All things you *didn't* give my husband a chance to do before you killed him. Your time is up."

Kat's mouth went dry, and the blood drained from her face.

What did *that* mean?

Jake stepped forward until the barrel of Peta's shotgun was pressing into his chest.

"Over my dead body," he growled.

"I wish." Peta narrowed her eyes but moved back so the four of them could exit the pantry. Dex stayed close to Mackenzie's heels, his hackles raised.

"We're not killing you." Bronwyn sniffed. "We're not murderers. Like you."

"Then threatening us with a gun is meaningless," Mackenzie pointed out.

"I didn't say I wouldn't wound you," Peta snapped back, her finger hazardously close to the trigger. "We're kicking you out. You have to leave Sanford and you're not welcome back. Ever."

"You can't do that!" Chloe cried.

"Watch us," Bronwyn smirked.

"It's better than you deserve," Mrs. White added. "Come on, move it. We don't have long."

"What's the hurry?" Jake asked.

"They don't want witnesses." Kat was only guessing,

but by the look on Mrs. White's face, she was correct. "Are you going to let us get our stuff?"

Their three captors shared a look, before Bronwyn shook her head. "We don't have time," she said brusquely.

Reluctantly, Kat submitted to being herded out of the Distillery, desperately scouting for someone, *anyone*, who might help them.

The area was deserted.

"Everyone is at The Strumpet, eating MREs we had conveniently put away." The smug smile Mrs. White flashed made Kat's teeth clench.

They exited the snow vestibule, and the cold slapped Kat in the face. It was late afternoon and daylight was already fading.

"You can't just throw us out without supplies," she protested. "We'll freeze to death."

"Not my problem," Peta replied. "You're wearing jackets and gloves, and we've got snowshoes for you." She pointed to the left, where four sets of snowshoes were leaning against the wall. "You've got five minutes to be out of my sight, otherwise I'm shooting."

"Kat!"

All heads swung towards the voice.

Cassie, Stephen, Sami, Jimmy and Lucas rounded the corner, coming to a standstill when they saw Peta. "What's going on?" Cassie's eyes were wide with confusion.

"Great." Bronwyn crossed her arms.

"The kids are already wearing snowshoes," Mrs. White pointed out. "Let's get rid of them, too. Fewer mouths to feed."

"No. Absolutely not." Kat crossed her own arms. "They've got nothing to do with this. Let them stay." Heart in her throat, she watched as Peta glanced first at Mrs. White, and then Bronwyn.

Resolved, Peta waved the teenagers over with the shotgun. "Looks like you've got yourselves mixed up with the wrong crowd." Peta's mouth was tight. "You've got five minutes."

No one moved.

"Time's ticking," Peta warned.

Cassie sidled up to Kat and pressed something covertly into her hand. Looking down, Kat realized it was a CB radio handset.

A flash of hope buoyed her, and she bent down to attach the snowshoes to her boots.

Taking her lead, the others followed suit, pulling on the snowshoes until they straightened and all looked at each other.

"Get going," Peta warned, a sadistic grin lighting her face.

"Fuck you, Peta." Kat turned and walked away. The snowshoes were ungainly and going to take some getting used to, but it was better than sinking into the snow and having to slog through it.

"Three minutes," Peta responded.

Kat kept walking, surrounded by her friends.

"What have you got up your sleeve, Kat?" Jake asked, when they had turned the corner out of sight.

"I'm assuming you have a plan?" Mackenzie matched her steps with Kat's. "Because it's not like you to have left without putting up a fight."

"What did you do to piss them off?"

Kat didn't like the accusatory tone in Stephen's voice.

She also didn't like how she was already puffing with

exertion, and they weren't even into the residential streets yet.

"Kat?" Mackenzie asked.

Kat stopped, propping her hands on her hips. She had a stitch in her side.

It had been days since she'd done one of Quinn's cardio workouts. Her body clearly missed them, and she missed bitching at him while she sweated.

She missed him, period.

"Cassie had this." Fumbling in her jacket pocket, she pulled out the radio. "We won't get far before it's dark, but we can spend the night in one of the houses on the edge of town—the guards don't patrol that far. And hopefully Quinn and the others won't be out of range, and we can radio them."

Chloe hugged Cassie, knocking the girl off her feet.

"Sorry! Sorry." Chloe laughed, pulling Cassie up. "But you're amazing! Where did you get your hands on it?"

"We found it at Nan's," Cassie said, dusting snow from herself. "We think it was Jez's, and he accidentally left it. See?" She reached for the handset, "It's a different model from the ones we've been using. And it was set to channel eighteen, and we never use that."

"If we keep it on eighteen, we might pick up chatter from Jez's group." Jake narrowed his eyes thoughtfully. "They must be within radio distance, or he wouldn't have been using it."

"Which means they're probably not at Arlington, or Greenville," Kat added. "Do you think we're too far from Arlington to reach Quinn and the others?"

"Depends what the range is," Jake replied. "Switch it to channel twenty-four and try."

Kat looked at the surrounding faces. "Everyone, cross your fingers."

DAY 64

Kat had slept fitfully, eager for dawn so they could get moving. The sooner they left Sanford, the closer they'd get to being within radio range of Quinn and the others.

The euphoric hope she'd felt yesterday when Jesse had responded on the radio had crashed and burned when she'd realized reception wasn't good enough to communicate with them.

She only hoped they'd heard enough of her warning, and weren't on their way back to Sanford. She didn't imagine Peta would be any friendlier to them.

With weak light creeping through the window of the house they'd stayed in, she turned on her side, wincing at an ache in her hip from laying on the bare floor. Chloe, who she'd been spooning, mumbled something in her sleep.

They were all lying packed tight together, making the most of each other's body heat. Like all the houses in Sanford, Townsend's scavenging crews had picked this one clean—not even the carpeted flooring remained.

Kat guessed she should be thankful Townsend hadn't taken the insulation from the roof. The house was freezing, but not the kind of freezing that was going to kill them.

As far as shelter went, they could have done worse.

There was rustling as someone got up, their stomach grumbling loud enough for Kat to hear. Sitting up, she saw it was Lucas. She didn't know him as well as she knew Cassie and Stephen, and hadn't spent the time with him she'd spent with Sami and Jimmy.

But he was a practical kid, cheeky, too. She liked him.

"Morning." He grinned at her. "I don't know about you, but I'm giving this accommodation a five star review on Yelp."

"I was only going to give them four stars. The lack of room service really sucks," Kat said, getting to her feet and stretching.

The others began stirring and sitting up, yawning and groaning.

Kat slipped away to the bathroom. Although the plumbing wasn't working, and there was no toilet paper, being able to pee on an actual toilet beat squatting in the snow. And it wasn't like they were going to be there long enough for the smell to become an issue.

She grimaced when she saw her reflection in the mirror. She'd never been overly conscious of her looks, but maintaining a beauty regime was her way of relaxing. It was her thing.

And, thanks to YouTube, she'd made a tonne of money filming herself trying out beauty products and putting on makeup. Like, a *lot* of money. All of which she'd donated to Rize Up, a charity supporting women and children fleeing domestic abuse.

She fingered her greasy hair, hanging limply around her face, and decided not to look at her eyebrows too closely. She was unrecognizable as the influencer whose viral video had sold out Glow Up concealer across the continental US.

What she wouldn't do for some concealer now. Hell, a toothbrush and some deodorant would make her cry.

She startled at a knock.

"Kat, are you nearly done?" Mackenzie asked through the closed door. "We're good to move out."

Kat stuck her tongue out at herself in the mirror. She

hadn't worn makeup in months, and Quinn seemed to like her just fine.

Now, she just had to get to him.

———

IT HAD TAKEN James and Jesse physically restraining him, to stop Quinn from heading back to Sanford straight away. Even with night falling and their precarious fuel gauges, he'd fought to leave.

Kat's broken message over the radio played on a loop in his head, making it impossible to sleep. Mike's constant pacing with an irritable Toby didn't help.

"I think he's finally down," Mike sighed, falling into the sofa next to Quinn.

Caught up in his own thoughts, Quinn hadn't realized the baby's fussing had quieted.

"Is he always like this?" He glanced over at the cot, afraid their voices would wake Toby.

"Lately, yeah." Mike's eyes were already closed.

No wonder the man looked like hell. Between a baby awake all night, and a kid awake all day...

"Hey! Hi there! Morning!" Gracie chirped, rolling out of a small bed pushed against the wall. "Yous are still here. How great!"

Mike grunted, but didn't open his eyes. "It's still early Mace, go back to sleep."

"Nuh uh. Yous is awake. And so's is Quinn. And it's morning already, see? The sun is coming up." She crossed the room and climbed into Mike's lap, patting at her father's ginger hair. "Toby didn't sleep much. Poor Daddy."

Rachel and James stirred under the blankets they were

sharing, and Quinn reached out a long leg to kick at Jesse's foot.

"Thanks for your hospitality, Mike. But it's time we got going." Quinn stood, restless impatience raging in his blood.

He had to get to Kat.

"You going to try find gas at that farmhouse on Twelve Mile Road I suggested?" Mike's eyes were still closed.

"Yes." Quinn kicked at Jesse again.

"And then what?" asked Rachel, sitting up. "It didn't sound like going back to Sanford was an option."

"Something obviously happened, and they had to leave Sanford," Quinn replied. "With no gas they're probably on foot. I think they'd go to the truck stop."

"You're right," James agreed, running a hand through his hair. "While we're here, should we check the town for any sign of Jez and Steph?"

"We don't have time. And Mike would know, right Mike?" Quinn looked at the exhausted man.

"I told you last night, anyone still left alive went with the Army when they came through. There's no one else here," Mike confirmed.

"And what about catching up with Jim and the others in Dutton?" Jesse asked. "You think we can get to the truck stop and then to Dutton in time?"

"We just need to head back toward Sanford. The closer we are, the more likely we'll be able to pick them up on the radio." Quinn rolled his shoulders, trying to ease the tension that gripped him. "Let's roll out, people."

HAVING FOUND enough gas at the farm Mike had told them about, the four of them wasted no time in re-tracing their tracks from yesterday.

The landscape was as white-washed and empty as ever, and Quinn thought again about moving somewhere warmer. He didn't know if they could survive another winter if this was their new reality. And even with Mike mentioning the Army, Quinn didn't think the military, or the government were going to be reinstating law and order again any time soon.

The world as they'd known it was gone.

Quinn closed his eyes briefly against the stinging wind, trying to ignore how hungry he was.

They'd gratefully accepted food from Mike last night, but hadn't wanted to stretch the hospitality to breakfast–the man had kids to think about. And while Quinn's head was onboard with this plan, his body was protesting. Loudly.

"Man, is that your *stomach*?" Jesse raised an eyebrow. They were stopped thirty miles from Arlington to try the radio again.

The need to make contact with Kat was a gnawing ache that Quinn couldn't shake. Raising a fist to rub against his chest he scowled at Jesse.

"Like you're not starving, too."

"I wanted to save these until we got back, but we may as well eat something." Rachel opened the backpack she'd picked up from the truck stop.

In the rush to get going this morning, Quinn had completely forgotten about her stashed supplies. He caught a protein bar she tossed at him and inhaled it in two bites.

"Here." She threw him a mini packet of pretzels. "It's not much, but it'll keep us going."

Making short work of the pretzels, Quinn pulled out the radio handset before pausing, suddenly hesitant to make the call. What if she didn't answer?

The uncertainty of not knowing what had happened

was a living beast within him that wanted to tear the world apart to reach her.

Could he handle radio silence? Or, worse, bad news?

"Q, you making the call?" Jesse asked.

Quinn turned his back and took two steps away.

"Kat, this is Quinn, standing by. Over." He held his breath, clutching tightly to the radio. "Kat, are you there? Over."

The seconds of silence ticked past, agonizingly slow.

"Kat, this is Quinn. Over."

The wind whistled through the bare branches of the trees they were parked beneath, the ever-present cold seeping deeper into his bones.

The static stretched, uninterrupted, and Quinn's head bowed. Surely they were close enough to be in range?

"Come on, we'll get closer and try again." James put his hand on Quinn's shoulder. "The clouds are low, they're probably blocking communication."

Quinn wanted to shrug the other man's concern away, but he swallowed and accepted the solidarity.

"Come on, let's move." His voice was gruff, and he avoided eye contact with James.

Walking back to the snowmobile Quinn pulled his shoulders back. There had always been the chance they were still too far out. Hope was not lost.

And then there was a crackle from the radio, and his heart stopped. Just, stopped beating. Stopped pumping blood, stopped being his life-force.

"Quinn?"

One word over the airwaves, and his heart continued to keep him alive. Blood rushed in his ears, and he struggled to hear over the thudding.

"Kat? Kat is that you? Over."

"Yes. God, Quinn. I've been trying to reach you all morning. Over."

"I'm here. Where are you? What happened?" In his haste to get information, Quinn forgot to say 'over'. "Just tell me you're okay. Over," he said, correcting his mistake.

"They kicked us out of Sanford, we spent the night in a house on the edge of town. We're going to make our way to a school bus depot that's a couple of miles away. We think we should get good traction in the snow with the deep treads on the tires. At least, that's what Jake thinks. Over."

"Who is with you? Over." Knowing his cousin was with her lightened some of the weight that Quinn carried.

"Jake and Mac, Chloe and Cassie, Stephen, Sami, Jimmy and Lucas. Over. Oh, and Dex. Over."

"Where do you plan to go? Over."

"We'll come to the safe house in Dutton. Isn't that where you're meeting up? Over."

"Yes. But with the snow it could take you a day or two to get there." The weight on his shoulders reasserted itself. "Driving on these roads is going to be dangerous. Over."

"Jake said we'll take it slow. But Quinn? When you meet up with Jim... you should know that Caroline knew they were banishing us. And she looked the other way. Over."

Rachel bumped Quinn's shoulder as she snatched the radio from him.

"What do you mean? Over."

"Rach? It's so good to hear you. Over."

"Kat! What do you mean, Caroline knew? Over."

"Jim has been telling people he and Caroline didn't agree with how we took back Sanford. And Caroline walked away instead of speaking up for us. You need to be careful with Jim. Over."

90

Quinn growled. Jim needed to be careful with *him*.

QUINN HADN'T BEEN in the rescue mission to Dutton when Mackenzie and the others had been taken by Gemma and her band of escaped prisoners, so the ravaged state of the town shocked him.

Although, given they were living through the apocalypse, nothing should shock him anymore. He slowed the snowmobile and coasted to a stop, Rachel and James doing the same. As Jesse was the only one of them who had been to the safe house, he and Quinn were swapping so Jesse could drive.

"What's with all the parked cars?" Quinn gestured to the deserted cars lining the road on both sides. "They don't have enough snow on them to have been parked here since the outbreak."

"You're right, they've been moved fairly recently," Rachel agreed, pressing herself into James' side. "How long is it going to take us to get there?"

"Not too long," Jesse said. "But these vehicles could be an issue. They're blocking the next right turn, which is the street I would have taken." He looked around, shielding his eyes from the sun reflecting off the snow. "I guess we keep going, and take the next available right."

"I don't like how noisy we are, whoever is still here knows where we are." Quinn's jaw ticked. He had a bad feeling about the place.

"Let's do this." Jesse switched the ignition, and the snowmobile roared to life. Tense and alert, Quinn climbed on behind.

Their progress was slow, because of the way vehicles were parked along the streets. Almost strategically.

The hairs on the back of Quinn's prickled. He didn't like how they were hemmed in, almost like they were being funneled...

"Jesse, stop!" Quinn thumped the other man's shoulder.

"Looks like an accident." Jesse pulled to a stop, but looking ahead Quinn realized it was because of the garbage truck blocking the road ahead, and not his warning.

"Turn around, we need to get out of here!" Even as Quinn yelled this, hooded figures appeared from the shadows between the buildings, encircling their idling snowmobiles.

They men were massive, and armed.

Quinn pulled his Ruger, even though he knew they were outgunned.

"Put it down. Hands up." A teen with a perky blonde ponytail stepped forward. She was unarmed, but Quinn instinctively knew this little cheerleader was running the show.

When he looked closer, he saw the hooded men weren't men at all. They looked like offensive linesmen from the local high school football team.

"Shit," he muttered under his breath, pocketing the handgun and raising his arms.

"Turn off the snowmobiles and get off. Slowly," Cheerleader commanded.

"We don't want any trouble," Rachel called out. "We're just on our way through."

"Well, we love trouble." Cheerleader grinned, all white teeth and dimples. "And this is our territory, so you can't pass through without paying your due."

"Your territory?" Quinn cocked his head. He couldn't believe they were getting jumped by a bunch of teenagers.

"From here to the Stratfield bridge is ours. Panther territory."

"Your parents around?" James asked, and was answered by the teen nearest him firing a bullet at the snow in front of him.

Well, that answered any questions about whether their weapons were actually loaded.

"What do you want?" Quinn mentally reviewed what was in their packs and what they could afford to part with. Jesse had said the safe house was fully stocked, but no one had been to check on it in weeks.

"We want it all." Cheerleader nodded at the kid to her left, who stepped forward. He was also blonde, and Quinn hated he couldn't see his eyes behind his reflective sunglasses.

"Sean, work your magic," she instructed, sweet as sugar.

"Alright boys, you heard Missy. Get to it," Sean said.

Quinn didn't want to be impressed at the coordinated and systematic way they approached taking everything, but they were a well-oiled machine. Clearly it wasn't their first time at staging this trap.

"At least leave us one snowmobile," Rachel protested.

"I'm doing you a favor. You keep heading in that direction and you'll be in Mallrat territory. You don't want to be heard by them, trust me. See you around." Missy winked. "Or not." She got on behind Sean on one of their snowmobiles and in seconds, they were gone. Just the echoing sound of the two-stroke engines as they disappeared, leaving Quinn and his friends with nothing.

CHAPTER SEVEN

Walking the couple of miles to the bus depot was easier said than done.

They were all drawing on reserves of endurance that were fast dwindling, and it showed in their slowing pace and gasping breaths.

Before all this, Kat had liked to joke she didn't exercise or jog because she'd watched enough *Law & Order* to know that's how you ended up finding a dead body.

Now, that wasn't so funny.

With over two feet of snow and empty bellies, it was tough going, even with the snowshoes. Without them, Kat didn't think they'd have made it.

When they finally saw the enormous outbuildings housing the yellow school buses in the distance, she allowed herself to fall backwards into the snow, grinning up at the sky.

"I was starting to think we'd never make it." Sami flopped down beside her, out of breath and red-cheeked. Jimmy landed beside her and the two joined hands.

Kat looked away.

Out of all of them, Cassie was the only one still on her feet. "Come on!" she called, continuing forward.

"I forgot she ran track. It's disgusting how fit she is," Kat grumbled.

"Tell me about it." Stephen groaned as he hoisted himself back to his feet. "But the sooner we get there, the sooner we find food."

Kat didn't want to think about what they'd do if there was nothing to eat. Their last meal had been the night before yesterday.

"I literally cannot go one step further." Chloe rolled over onto her stomach and cradled her head in her hands. "I'm going to nap, and you bring me some food. Okay?"

"Come on, sis. Let's get moving." Jake pulled at Chloe's arms until she reluctantly stood.

"I don't want to." She pouted, but began trudging forward, Dex faithfully at her side.

Sighing, Kat joined Jake and Mackenzie and they followed after her.

"How did Jimmy know about this place?" Mackenzie asked.

"Yeah, I thought the bus depot was out near the quarry," Jake said.

"Jimmy's dad works construction. Worked." Kat paused. "Anyway, he was on a crew building the sheds. They only finished and relocated a week or so before the outbreak, which is probably why it wasn't on Townsend's radar. Otherwise for sure he'd have requisitioned the buses."

"And you're sure we'll be able to drive a bus through snow this deep?" Mackenzie was frowning at the ground.

"The bigger and heavier the bus, the better the traction," Jake replied, slinging an arm over her shoulder. "Bus tires are made to grip in these conditions. And there'll be snow chains we can attach."

Sweat prickled on the back of Kat's neck as she realized this may not be as simple as hopping onto a bus and driving into the sunset.

"We'll figure it out." Jake squeezed Mackenzie closer and loneliness bloomed in Kat. It wasn't even about Quinn; it was about missing Mackenzie now that she'd found her forever person. Rachel, too.

Kat curled her lip at herself. What kind of person begrudged her best friends their happiness? Her. She did. The oily feeling swirled in her gut, as if to remind her of exactly who she was.

God, she'd kill for some wine right now.

If it was a choice between a glass of chilled pinot grigio, and a hamburger with the lot—she'd still take the alcohol. She'd rather be numb, than full.

It had been hours since her last drink, and the tremors were starting up. She swallowed against a rising nausea and pulled her shoulders back. She could do this.

She'd fallen behind, and was the last of their group to arrive. Cassie and Stephen were already coming out of the demountable building that had been set up as the operations office, and their dejected faces told her everything she needed to know.

There was no food here.

Not that she'd expected a hamburger, but Kat's hollow stomach twisted in disappointment.

"Good news, or bad news?" Jimmy called out, striding from the adjacent outbuilding.

No one answered him.

Unperturbed, Jimmy came to a stop in front of them.

"Good news, all the gear we need to drive one of these

babies in the snow is here and they look to be fueled up. Bad news, they haven't been started in months, so the batteries are dead."

"Well, that can't be too hard, right?" Jake stepped forward, and Kat had never been happier that Jake was a mechanic. He'd sort this. "These buses are manual transmission. If we can't find a portable jump-starter, we'll just have to do a push-start."

Kat and Chloe exchanged a look. Kat didn't know what a push-start was, and she wasn't sure she wanted to find out.

They all traipsed to the row of lined-up school buses, leaving their snowshoes at the entrance to the shed. It was like an enormous hanger, with yellow lines on the concrete floor delineating bays for each of the buses.

The relief of not having to push her way through snow as she walked left Kat lightheaded.

Or maybe that was hunger?

Either way, she needed to sit down.

"See? The chains are in tubs." Jimmy opened the storage compartment on the side of one of the buses.

"Okay, everyone start to lay the chains out on the ground to separate and straighten them," Jake instructed. "Make sure the crosslinks are facing up. I'm going to look for a jump-starter."

They were finished with the chains long before Jake finally managed to crank the battery and get the bus powered up. Kat was just grateful she didn't have to discover how you push-started a bus.

Once they'd hung the chains over the back tires, Jake reversed so the ends of the chains cleared the front of the tires. After locking the links together and hooking the outside of the chains as tight as possible, they started the process all over again on the front tires.

While last-minute checks were being made, Kat headed back outside and over to the office building. She was hoping to find maps of the region and her mouth tipped up in a half grin when she found a whole wall covered in them. After taking down the ones she thought might be useful she stared over at a bench, where a dispatch radio sat.

She wished she knew if it would be helpful to bring with them, but the truth was, she had no idea how these kinds of things worked. She decided to file the information away, in case it could be handy in the future.

Right now, they needed to get moving. The hours of daylight were fading fast.

TRAVELLING in the bus was agonizingly slow. And Chloe's obvious distress wasn't helping matters. She was curled over in her seat, rocking.

"Chlo, come on. You need to get it together," Jake called over his shoulder from the driver's seat.

Kat slid onto the seat beside Chloe and put her arm around her shoulders.

"What is it?" She rubbed at Chloe's upper arm. "We're going to be okay, you know that, right?"

"It's Ash." Chloe raised a tear-stained face. "He won't know where to find me if I'm not in Sanford."

Kat's eyes welled in sympathy. She didn't know what to say.

Chloe didn't want to hear that her husband was likely never coming back to her, and if by some chance he did? She was right. He wouldn't know where to look.

"I'm so sorry." The softly spoken words were all she could manage.

"Woah, look at that!" Lucas had his face pressed against

the window, looking out into the field they were driving past. Sami and Jimmy joined him, and Kat had to crane her neck to see what he was talking about.

"What the hell?" Jake slowed the bus and then stopped completely.

Everyone was staring with open mouths.

An enormous Boeing 737 was lying on top of the snow. While the underside was buried, there was only a light dusting of snow along the top.

"That hasn't been there for very long, has it?" Kat breathed. She rubbed at the fog she'd caused against the glass, sure that when she looked again, the incongruous sight would have disappeared.

Nope. The giant-ass airplane was still stranded in an otherwise empty field.

"What is it doing there?" Mackenzie asked.

"I've never seen one up so close before," said Jimmy. "Can we check it out?"

"Hell yes!" Lucas punched the air. "I've never flown before." His face fell. "Probably never going to, now."

"It doesn't look like it crashed, but there could be passengers who need help." Kat shrugged, already standing.

"Hang on a minute!" Jake raised his voice to be heard over the excited chatter of the teenagers. "We don't know why it landed there, or where it's come from. There could be infected people onboard."

"But we're immune," Kat pointed out. She was already envisioning the tiny bottles of alcohol you got on flights. "And there could be food onboard," she added.

That cinched it. They were out of the bus and strapping on their snowshoes in minutes.

The cold shouldn't have been a shock, but after the bliss

of sitting in a heated bus, it was a harsh reminder of their reality.

Kat winced, her eyes tearing up in the freezing air.

The closer they got to the 737 the larger it loomed, until it blocked out all else and they stood before it, awed.

"How did it get here?" Cassie wondered out loud.

"Ah, it flew." Lucas bumped his shoulder into Cassie, and the two laughed.

The door to the 737 was closed, and there were no obvious tracks of anyone having disembarked.

"You think there's anyone still in there?" Jake said.

"Only one way to find out." Kat took a step forward, eyeing the mechanical latch on the door. Because of the angle the airplane had landed and the built-up snow it had burrowed into, she only had to stand on her tip-toes to reach the handle.

"Hang on, won't it be pressurized?" Chloe called out.

"That's only when it's in the air," Jake replied. "Kat should be able to rotate the handle and pull it open."

Without stopping to second guess herself, Kat followed Jake's instructions and the heavy door opened easily, swinging out and across.

She jumped back and then stood motionless.

Nothing happened.

"Um. Hello?" she called out.

There was no sound from inside. The others shuffled behind her and Kat strained to hear. "Hello?" she tried again.

"Want me to give you a leg up?" Jake asked, appearing at her side.

"Do you think... I mean, they're probably not alive in there, are they?" Kat rubbed her gloved hands on her pant legs.

"Like you said, only one way to find out." Jake tipped his chin at her. "Want me to go in first?"

"No, I got this." Where her courage was coming from, Kat had no idea. She just knew she could do this. She fitted her foot into Jake's clasped hands and he hoisted her so she could swing herself through the doorway.

"Wait!"

Kat froze at Chloe's voice, one foot still dangling.

"What if they're hostile? And armed?" Chloe reached for Kat's leg. "It's not worth it. Let's just go."

"My spidey senses says it's okay," Kat called back to Chloe as she drew her foot up and got to her feet.

The interior was gloomy, lit only by faded light coming through partially opened window shades. As Kat's eyes adjusted, she scanned the space but didn't see any people. Hesitantly, she stepped further down the aisle, picking up pace the further she went. Row after row of passenger seats were empty.

The air smelled stale and tickled Kat's nose until she sneezed.

She heard Jake climb in behind her, but didn't turn around until she'd reached the end of the plane and checked the rear galley and the two tiny toilet cubicles.

There was no one onboard.

She made her way back up the front, noting that all the head rest covers were straight and none of the tray tables were out of place.

"There's no one here." She shrugged at Jake.

"No one in the cockpit, either."

"So, it's empty?"

"Looks that way." Jake squatted at the door so he could speak to the others. "Come on up."

One by one they jumped up, until it was just Lucas, and

Jake and Stephen pulled him in. Dex stayed on the ground, whining.

"This is so cool." Lucas beamed at them, before launching himself into one of the premium seats. "And cushy as hell!"

"Any food?" Mackenzie asked.

"I haven't checked yet, but the back galley had some ovens," Kat replied. "You know, with the way those clouds are looking, we're going to get more snow this afternoon. Maybe it wouldn't be a bad idea to stay here for the night?"

"Better than sleeping in the bus." Lucas stretched his legs out and leaned back, putting his hands behind his head. "Like I said, this is cushy."

"There's food!" Cassie's excited screech carried the length of the aircraft, and Kat grinned. Things were looking up.

———

QUINN DIDN'T KNOW the last time he'd been this furious.

A couple of teenagers had jumped them and they'd lost not just their supplies, but their transport, too.

That wasn't the worst of it.

Losing the radio meant he couldn't touch base with Kat. The need to communicate with her was twisting his gut. He hadn't realized how much security he'd placed in the ability to contact her. And without it? He was ready to tear the world apart.

Thighs burning from the slog through the snow, he growled in frustration.

"Would you stop with the caveman noises?" Rachel complained, coming to a stop with her hands on her hips.

"No one is thrilled with the situation, but look on the bright side. We haven't seen any of these Mallrats."

"What kind of name is that, anyway?" Quinn grumbled.

"Think it's worth trying the houses for food?" Jesse asked, looking around at the white picket fences that lined the street.

The houses they'd already checked had been picked over, and encountering the inevitable dead bodies of the inhabitants wasn't something Quinn was keen to keep repeating.

Thankfully, the cold weather had slowed the decomposition process and inhibited the stench Quinn had been expecting, but coming across people dead in their homes wasn't a pleasant experience.

He'd prefer they keep walking. It's not like they were starving.

"It's going to snow soon. We should keep going," he said.

"Q, we don't all have tree trunks for legs, like you. I need a rest." Jesse was at the head of their single file line, breaking the way for them. They'd been swapping out leaders and taking turns in doing the hard work, but they only really made headway when Quinn was forging the path.

"I'll take lead." It had been less than half an hour since he'd taken his turn, but Quinn didn't mind. At least at the front he knew they were going as fast as they could. Walking behind someone else was driving him crazy.

"We can't keep going in the dark, especially if snow is coming." James held out a hand, as though expecting Quinn's protest. "We should find a house to spend the night, even if it doesn't have food."

"Preferably one without dead bodies." Rachel wrinkled her nose.

Quinn's jaw ticked, but he knew they outnumbered him.

"Fine," he ground out. Just because he'd agreed, didn't mean he had to be gracious about it. "Which one?" The houses on this street were cookie-cutter look-alikes, with nothing to distinguish one from the other.

"Eenie meenie miini moh..."

Quinn didn't wait for Jesse to finish his damn nursery rhyme, and instead began making his way to the closest house. Unlatching the front gate he tunneled a path to the front door and didn't bother knocking before trying the handle. Unlocked.

Didn't look like it had been forced open, though. So maybe it hadn't been targeted by scavengers. Yet.

Stamping the snow from his boots he stepped inside, stopping to sniff. You could tell the air was old by the musty smell; and by the scent, no one had been in this house for a long while.

Dust coated the surfaces, and by the looks of things, the inhabitants had left in a hurry. Mold-covered plates sat on the kitchen table, with a jug of juice that was green and a bowl of desiccated fruit.

The contents of a handbag lay scattered on the floor, beside a pair of expensive-looking high heels that lay on their side.

Quinn went straight for the pantry, knowing from experience to stay well clear of the refrigerator.

And hallelujah, it was stocked. Jars of olives, fancy pink salt and boxes of gourmet crackers. Ruthlessly organized, there were rows of labeled plastic tubs with rice, pasta, pumpkin seeds, muesli, nuts... whoever had lived here had a taste for the finer foods.

Jackpot.

DAY 65

"Ah, nothing like fresh powder," James joked, staring out the window of the house the next morning.

"Quit procrastinating and help us load up this food." Rachel spared him a glance over her shoulder, before continuing to cram food into reusable Whole Foods shopping bags. "After having looked through this woman's wardrobe, I'm not surprised she shopped at Whole Foods."

"I didn't think Dutton had a Whole Foods?" Jesse looked up from his own packing.

"They don't. She must have gone to the city."

"She drove to Chicago to get her groceries?" Jesse snorted. "Some people have way too much money."

"Sy-V didn't care about money," Quinn said quietly from his seat at the kitchen bench. "Being wealthy didn't save her." He tightened Kat's scarf around his neck, breathing in her scent.

"I still think about our immunity, and what it means." Jesse stood up, slinging a bag over his shoulder. "What do you think the mutations are that Mike mentioned? Should we be worried about this military group, or trying to hook up with them and find out more about this colony?"

Rachel stood, too. "You know that Chloe won't go to a colony, right? Not when there's a chance Ash might come home." She studied Jesse intently. "You have feelings for her, don't you?"

"Would it be a problem if I did?" Jesse asked carefully.

"You're okay with her carrying other man's baby?"

"I'd raise it as my own," he replied firmly.

"Are you going to tell her how you feel?" Rachel cocked an eyebrow.

"It's too soon, she's still grieving. I want to give her time."

Rachel nodded approvingly. "Good call."

Quinn wondered if Jesse knew he'd be taking on all four women if he started something with Chloe. They were as close as sisters and came as a package deal.

The grin on James' face said he understood what Jesse was getting himself in for.

"Are we finished this heart-to-heart? Because we should get moving." Quinn said from his seat at the kitchen's island bench. "It's going to take us all day to walk to the safehouse, and if the others will wonder where we are if they get there before us."

"You're right, they'll freak if we're not there," Rachel said. "Let's go."

Outside, the streets of Dutton were quiet. Serene, even.

The fresh dump of snow amplified the emptiness of the town. Quinn had to keep reminding himself it was not, in fact, empty. Dutton was apparently home two rival gangs, and he would very much like to avoid contact with either of them.

"Are we taking this left, or the next?" he called back to Jesse, who was in charge of directions.

"This one," Jesse confirmed.

Quinn was sweating beneath his layers, and he stopped to drink the water they'd made from snow they had melted and boiled last night.

"Check that out." He pointed to a disturbance in the snow next to them.

"Are they animal tracks?" Rachel asked, moving over to

them. "It's dog prints, and lots of them. Looks like a sizable pack."

Quinn swore under his breath. Just what they needed—rabid pets-turned-strays. They could use their weapons if attacked, but the sound of gunshots would carry. Who knew what that could attract?

"Wait, do you hear that?" He cocked his head to the side, listening intently. "Not a two-stroke, I think it's a vehicle."

The distant rumbling was getting steadily closer.

"We need cover!" James turned in a circle, surveying their options.

"They'll just follow our path. There's no hiding." Quinn pulled out his Ruger and dropped to a knee, facing the oncoming threat. "Get in a defensive position."

The others flanked him and together they waited—tense and alert—as the sound got louder, closer, the path they'd forged through the snow a beacon leading straight to them.

"Is that..." Quinn squinted.

"It's a school bus!" Rachel cried. "Do you think it's them?"

"Maybe, maybe not." Jesse glanced at the map he was carrying. "I would have expected them to take a different route to the safehouse."

Chest tight, Quinn strained to make out any detail on the bus as it drew nearer, but the glare of the sun on the snow made it impossible. When the bus was still three hundred feet away, it came to a stop and the passenger slowed slowly swung open.

"Quinn!" It was Kat, and she was half stumbling and half running and everything in Quinn zeroed in on this one small woman, fighting her way through the snow towards him. His heart felt like it had doubled in size—straining against the confines of his ribcage and making him struggle to draw in enough oxygen.

And then he was striding towards her, catching her around the waist when she was only steps from the door and backing her until he had her pinned against the side of the bus.

He was oblivious to anyone and everything. The Panthers could come, or the Mallrats. Hell, the military could show up, but right now, Quinn only had eyes for the woman in his arms.

Her legs wrapped around his hips and her hands tangled in his beard and her sweet voice was chanting his name, over and over again.

His mouth crashed down on hers, swallowing her cries as he claimed her, teeth clashing and tongues dueling. She was *everything*. When they finally broke apart, panting, he cupped her face and gazed into her eyes. He was both lost, and found.

There was no coming back from this.

"We couldn't reach you on the radio. I didn't know what had happened," she said, biting at her lower lip. "I've been so worried." She buried her face in the side of his neck, her hands clutching at his jacket. Pulling him closer.

"I'm here, darlin'. I'm here."

And he was never letting her go again.

CHAPTER EIGHT

DAY 66

They had celebrated their arrival at the safehouse with wine late into the night, and by the time Kat and Quinn had fallen into bed, he'd been snoring in seconds.

Lying on her stomach in his arms now, with the morning light soft, the fireplace still burning low and having had access to both toothpaste *and* deodorant, Kat was content. The events of the last forty-eight hours seemed hazy, now that she was warm and safe.

Although there was still the matter of Steph being missing, and Jim and Caroline betraying them. And she knew Quinn had noticed how much alcohol she'd consumed–he was going to bring that up for sure. It actually surprised her he hadn't already called her out on being a high-functioning alcoholic.

Not that she *was* an alcoholic. She could understand how someone might get that impression, but she had it totally under control. She could stop any time she wanted.

But come on, giving up alcohol during an apocalypse was a terrible idea.

"What are you thinking?" His bare chest under her hand vibrated as he growled his question, softening it with the tip of his finger that he ran down the furrow between her eyebrows.

She turned her head on the pillow and met his eyes.

"Morning, handsome."

"Darlin', are you worried about something?"

"Ah, yes. We slept together last night, and you didn't once try to ravish me."

His gravelly laugh shot straight to her lady parts, and her thighs clenched.

He flipped her onto her back and she reveled in the weight he draped over her. But it wasn't enough. He was holding back, using his thighs and elbows to take the brunt of his body weight.

And she wanted it *all*.

Wrapping her arms as far around his middle as she could, she pressed her open palms into the smooth skin of his back. He countered by lowering himself further, his delicious bulk dwarfing her.

"Having sex with me, especially the first time, isn't something you do when under the influence," he cautioned, his face serious.

"Why?" She arched her back until there was not a sliver of space between them, sure he could feel her throbbing heart.

"You feel how big I am?" He rolled his hips gently.

Kat's body burst into flames as liquid heat coursed through her. She whimpered, desperate. Even through his boxer briefs, his cock was thick and hard. And big.

The need to know just *how* big had Kat panting.

"So..."

"So we take this slow." His lips found the sensitive skin behind her ear, ghosting down to press open-mouthed kisses along the column of her throat. "I appreciate the lack of clothes, darlin'."

She shivered, tipping her head back to allow him access and immensely pleased with herself for having the foresight to sleep naked.

"I aim to please."

He growled in response, and she was in very real danger of getting addicted to the sound.

"So do I." He moved down her body, settling himself between her spread thighs and cupping her breasts, the roughened pads of his thumbs teasing her taut nipples.

She moaned, pushing herself further into his hands.

"More."

"So greedy," he murmured, lowering his head and sucking one nipple and then the other into his mouth. He licked and nipped and suckled, his hands plumping her flesh, driving her ever higher with his exquisite torture.

The rub of his beard, the hint of his teeth and the heat of his tongue had her head thrashing on the pillow. She was going to *explode* if he didn't get to her vagina right. fucking. now.

"Quinn. I need... I need..."

She was beyond coherent thought.

"Please," she begged.

"You need this?" He kissed his way down her stomach, his big hands going between her thighs to spread them exposing her most intimate parts to him fully.

"So pretty," he praised, eyes hooded and hungry.

Of its own volition, her hand dropped to her clit, fingers circling and hips bucking.

"Uh uh, darlin'." He took both her hands in one of his large ones, pinning them to the sheets at her side.

She moaned in frustration and then stilled–eyes closed– as she felt the softness of his beard rasp against the tender skin between her thighs. And then his mouth closed over her soaked center, and his growl rumbled through her pussy. She wrenched a hand from his grasp and stuffed her fist in her mouth, biting down to keep her scream inside.

The intensity and dedication of his focus as he worshipped her had stars bursting behind Kat's eyelids, the rush of her orgasm taking her breath away. Slack and satiated, her head fell back, and she licked at her dry lips.

Quinn pulled back to blow on her over-sensitized clit and then continued his carnal assault with first one thick finger, and then two, pushing inside her slickness. She jolted, clenching around the welcome intrusion and burying her hands in his hair, urging him on. His tongue swirled and lapped at her nub while his fingers plundered, and another orgasm ripped through her, causing her whole body to shudder.

With one last lick, Quinn lifted his head like a conquering warrior, wiping the back of his hand over his mouth. Feral. Primal.

Kat almost came again.

She stared at him, wide-eyed and not sure anything could top that as a sexual experience. Not even sex.

"You still okay?" he asked, coming up to lie at her side, face-to-face.

"I am so much better than okay." She was practically purring.

"Good. Because I need you well prepped."

Just how big *was* he?

Getting out of the bed he pulled a condom and a small tube of lubrication from the pocket of his hoodie. Had he been carrying those this whole time?

"I don't think I need that." She eyed the lube. She'd never been this wet in her life.

"Trust me." And then he pushed down his boxer briefs, stomach muscles flexing enticingly.

Kat swallowed. His cock was enormous.

It jutted out proudly–thickly veined and lengthy. Kat had honestly never seen a dick this size. Not even on PornHub.

Quinn ran his hand up its length, his thumb flicking at the pearl of pre-cum at the tip.

His eyes trained on hers, he stepped closer to the bed. "We don't have to do anything you're not comfortable with."

"What does that mean, exactly?"

"It means I realize I'm... a lot to take."

She licked her lips, her heart beat skipping when she saw the flash of desire in his eyes.

Sitting up, she scooted closer to the edge of the mattress until she was eye level with his monster of a cock. There was no way she was getting that whole thing in her mouth, but damn she was going to have fun trying.

"You sure about this?" Quinn widened his stance, one hand on his hip and the other casually cupping his balls.

In answer, Kat leaned forward and licked up the length of his cock, twirling her tongue at the tip to savor his salty taste. Opening her mouth wide, she slid down the thick shaft until her eyes watered, and then came back up, gasping.

His hand tangled in her hair, undemanding, but she

dove back down for more, obsessed with getting him as far down her throat as she could manage.

"Kat, darlin'..." He groaned and rocked back on his heels, removing himself from her needy grasp. "If you keep that up, I'm a goner."

Swiftly sheathing himself with the condom, he lifted his chin at her. "Lie back, darlin'. I'm going to make this good for you."

His promise had a hot flush sweeping her body, and Kat complied readily. She wasn't sure how her body was going to accept his size, but she knew with unwavering certainty he would never hurt her.

The mattress dipped as he kneeled above her, a god among men.

"I want you to keep your legs on the inside of mine," he instructed, lowering himself over her and straddling her with his powerful thighs. "It's like missionary, but by keeping your legs closed you get to control how much depth I give you."

She nodded, welcoming his weight as he lay on top of her, supported only by his forearms either side of her head.

She was beyond ready for him.

He kissed her then, passion and yearning swirling into a potent mix within her. She could taste her own spicy sweetness on him which just made her burn brighter. Hotter.

When he shifted and positioned himself at the entrance of her pussy, she moaned and tilted her pelvis, seeking whatever he had to give her.

The blunt head of his cock was wide and slippery, making her realize at some point he'd used the lube. It notched and he paused, until with a push of his hips he was stretching her wide, his cock filling her up.

It was unlike anything she'd felt before; an ache

conquered by the satisfied burn of pain. But it was good pain. So, so good.

"More," she breathed, opening her legs fractionally.

Holding himself in check, he stared down at her.

"Are you sure?"

"Fuck me, Quinn." She punctuated her statement by widening her legs further.

"I want you to touch yourself. Get that little clit of yours all swollen and juicy."

The moment she circled that sensitive bundle of nerves an orgasm was upon her; the combination of Quinn's giant cock filling her and the stimulation of her clit enough to send her spinning into oblivion.

When she finally regained her senses she was rocking her hips to a rhythm set by Quinn, his controlled thrusts pushing past pain until there was nothing but pure, undiluted pleasure.

She was surrounded and filled by this man; his scent, his labored breathing, his hands carefully cupping her face as he fucked into her. Again, and again.

"You need to let go," she gasped. "*Fuck me*, Quinn. Hard."

There was an infinitesimal suspension as he processed her permission, and then he buried his face between her neck and shoulder and proceeded to destroy her with each deep push, driving into her at a pace she had no hope of matching.

Instead, she lay there and exulted in the glorious annihilation of her heart. Fingernails clinging to his broad shoulders, she allowed herself to admit she was in love with this man.

He came with a shout, his giant body stilling over hers.

And, impossibly, Kat's pussy tightened and her body wrung yet another orgasm from her.

She closed her eyes, and let it take her.

————

QUINN SLUMPED TO HIS SIDE, conscious of getting his weight off Kat's tiny form. She was boneless in his arms as he rolled to his back and brought her with him, until she draped across his chest.

"I'm just going to have a little nap." She nuzzled into his chest, her fingers winding through his chest hair and kneading like a kitten.

His arms tightened around her. There was no way Quinn could sleep after the earth shattering revelation of sex with this woman. It was beyond anything he'd ever imagined, and he'd imagined plenty.

He was reeling, physically and emotionally, after the most intense climax he'd experienced. The way she'd responded to his touch, giving him everything...

He'd never had a woman trust him so implicitly in the bedroom.

Kat made a sleep-sound, and he realized she really had fallen asleep. He grinned.

He pulled the blankets over them both as his heart rate calmed. The old farmhouse was a brilliant option as a safe-house. Not only did every bedroom and living space have its own fireplace, but when the others had first found it and spent time here, they'd fully stocked it with everything they could need–including at least a month's worth of firewood.

Beneath the covers, Quinn trailed his fingers up and down Kat's back, still not quite believing he could touch her like this.

She'd been an unattainable dream for so long, and now she was lying in his arms.

It felt like forever since they'd left Sanford, and yet, no time at all. Regardless, everything had changed. If their home was no longer safe, they had to reevaluate.

And when Jim arrived, he had some things to answer for.

Quinn had put on hold his questions for Kat about Jim, but her grace period was over. The need to know what exactly was between them could impact their entire group.

There was a knock at their door, and Kat started awake.

"Breakfast is up!" Someone called out.

As if on cue, Kat's stomach rumbled.

"Come on, darlin'. You need food." He kissed the top of her head.

She grumbled but sat up, her perky breasts bouncing and distracting him completely. In seconds he'd rolled her onto her back and was devouring her tits like a man possessed.

Like a starving man who'd found his manna. Breakfast could wait.

THE MIRACLES KEPT ON COMING, with actual eggs for breakfast. Seating himself at the kitchen table and pulling Kat into his lap, Quinn looked around at the others.

Everyone was here, relaxed and warm and well-fed. Dex lay on the floor beneath everyone's feet, thumping his tail occasionally to contribute to the conversation.

"Do I even ask how you got these?" he asked, accepting a plate of fried eggs from Mackenzie.

"You can, but that means I get to ask about this." She

waved a hand between him and Kat, waggling her eyebrows. "Is this a thing now?"

"It's a thing," Kat confirmed, picking up a fork to start on the eggs.

"About time." Jake grinned, leaning over to slap Quinn on the shoulder.

"Do we need to talk to you about protection?" Cassie hid a cheeky grin behind a mug.

Kat didn't seem perturbed by the attention and Quinn couldn't help his own grin. He loved he could sit here with his girl, laughing with their friends.

"So, the eggs?" Kat asked, as she casually fed him a mouthful over her shoulder.

"The last time we were here we set up a free-range coop in the backyard." Mackenzie said. "We didn't know if the chickens would survive, but they have."

"And do we have enough stored firewood to continue to keep the house this warm?" Quinn asked. He hadn't even bothered to put on a sweater when they'd come downstairs—all he needed was his undershirt and a long-sleeve Henley.

"Enough to last out the winter," Jake confirmed. "How long do we plan on staying here?"

There was silence as everyone looked at each other.

"I don't know about you, but this sure beats The Strumpet." Lucas leaned back, tipping his chair onto the back two legs. "And it's not like they'll take us back, anyway."

"You still haven't told us what you did to get kicked out." Stephen narrowed his eyes at Kat, and Quinn was instantly on the defensive. He hated when people assumed the worst of her.

He wasn't stupid; he knew Kat was messy and disorganized, that she was easily distracted and sometimes let others down. But she was also magic; kind and funny and charismatic and loyal. He didn't expect her to be perfect, and it aggravated him when others did.

"Back off, kid," he growled.

"It's a valid question, though," Rachel countered. "What happened after we left?"

"Nothing!" Chloe said. "We were taking inventory of the pantry and Bronwyn and Mrs. White barged in, and then Peta was pointing a gun at us."

"What about Caroline? I thought she was involved?" James asked, looking to Kat.

Quinn's hand tightened on Kat's thigh, only releasing when she twined her fingers with his.

"Let's get one thing straight, while we're all here. This wasn't Kat's fault." He stared hard at each person present. "So you need to stop casting blame her way."

"I just can't believe that Jim and Caroline would betray us." Rachel held up a hand when Quinn's jaw ticked. "I'm not saying it's Kat fault. It's just, a shock. And it's going to be awkward when he turns up here."

"At the risk of being called a fuckboy again, I think Kat needs to explain the animosity between her and Jim," said James. His mention of the nickname Kat had given him when he'd returned to Sanford had her sticking out her tongue at him.

"That's none of your business," she replied.

"It kind of is." Chloe spoke softly, but she had everyone's attention. "If it has anything to do with why Caroline didn't stand up for us, then it affects us all."

Kat squirmed uncomfortably in his lap.

"It's nothing," she muttered.

Quinn had assumed Rachel, Chloe and Mackenzie would already know. He didn't think the four of them kept any secrets from each other. The fact they didn't know was... interesting.

"You know what? It's actually not my business." Cassie stood up from the table, casting a sympathetic glance at Kat. "Come on." She grabbed Stephen's hand and looked to Sami, Jimmy and Lucas. "We can go and... do something."

When the five of them filed out, expectant gazes landed on Kat.

She cleared her throat, fiddling with the fork.

"It's not a big deal, and it's in the past. I don't even think Caroline knows, and Jim and I pretend it never happened."

"Pretend *what* never happened?" Every protective instinct in Quinn screamed to life, and his teeth ground together.

The girls traded confused looks.

"How do we not know about this?" Mackenzie asked.

Kat's back straightened, and she took a deep breath. Quinn felt each of her movements as though she were a part of him.

"We had a thing, okay? When I was at school."

Chloe gasped, and Rachel reached to clutch at Mackenzie's hand.

"When you were at school..." Quinn's voice was low, controlled. "When you were a teenager and he was, what? How old would he have been?"

"It wasn't like that."

Quinn shifted her in his lap so he could see her face. When she ducked her head, his fingers tipped her chin so he could make eye contact.

"How old were you?" His voice was gruff, but not accusatory.

"Fifteen," she whispered.

"And he was an adult, and a person in a position of power. He was the football coach then, right?"

"Honey, why didn't you tell us?" Chloe's eyes were brimming with tears. "He abused you."

"No! It wasn't like that," Kat protested. "I wasn't abused, it was completely consensual." She lowered her eyes. "And I couldn't tell you because I knew it was wrong."

"It *was* wrong, but that's on him, not you," Rachel said. "Honey, this wasn't your fault."

"It was my fault," Kat whispered. "I knew he was married, and I wanted him anyway."

When tears began sliding down Kat's cheeks, Quinn was suddenly engulfed by the girls throwing their arms around Kat, their unwavering solidarity the only thing keeping him from committing violence.

How *dare* Jim use a young girl that way? It was despicable for him to have preyed on a schoolgirl, and for it to have been Kat... the urge to cause damage and destruction rode him hard.

"Okay, enough." Kat sniffled and pushed the girls away. "I could really use a drink after that."

Chloe shook her head and dove back in for another hug. "Not a chance. You think we haven't noticed how much you've been drinking?"

"She's right, Kat." Rachel put a hand on Kat's shoulder. "You need to cut back, before it gets out of hand."

"It's not a problem," Kat huffed.

"So you won't mind giving me the mini bottles of liquor you found on the airplane, then?" Mackenzie asked, eyebrow raised.

"You're such a bitch." Kat pouted. "Fine, you can have them."

"But now that you've mentioned it, can we talk about

this airplane?" Jesse asked, bringing the coffeepot over to the table.

"I'm more interested in what you heard about the military and possible mutations to the virus," Jake said.

Quinn appreciated them taking the heat away from Kat, but it didn't detract from the fury that had settled in his gut.

Jim's reckoning was coming.

CHAPTER NINE

Kat felt light. Lighter than she had in years. The weight of that secret had taken its toll, with the oily feeling so much a part of her daily life that it was shocking to be free of it.

But the unconditional love from her friends and lack of judgement from Quinn soothed at the hollow inside her that had been grooved out by the constant weight of that guilt.

She still blamed herself, of course. The whole illicit affair with Jim would never have happened if she hadn't pursued him. But, with the hindsight of time, she could understand that he also had a part to play. He'd broken vows and encouraged her infatuation.

"I'm putting on another pot of coffee." James stood up from the kitchen table, his hand touching Kat lightly on the shoulder as he walked by. "We should get the teens back in here. We need to talk about what we're going to do."

"I'll get them, I need to go to the bathroom anyway," Kat said, slipping from Quinn's lap and giving him a quick peck on his bearded cheek. "Thank you," she whispered in his ear.

"I've got you, darlin'. Always."

A warm glow set up residence in Kat's heart, and she went to find the teens with a light step. They were spread out in the living room and Kat picked up a cushion and threw it at Sami and Jimmy, who were making out on the sofa.

"Quit it, you two. It's too early for those kind of shenanigans," she scolded.

"Don't try to adult us, Kat." Jimmy grinned and threw the cushion back. "It was literally last week you were asking us what we wanted to be when we grew up, because you were looking for ideas."

"Aren't you like, mega famous on YouTube?" Lucas asked. "I heard you raked it in for making videos putting on eyeshadow and shit."

"Oh my god, her channel is *so* much more than that!" Cassie exclaimed. She held a cushion to her chest and turned to Kat. "I had a notification set for whenever a new video dropped. You changed my life."

Stephen scoffed. "How?"

"Do you *remember* how awful my foundation was in freshman year? If it hadn't been for Kat, I would never have learned to blend. And don't get me started on her tips for contouring."

"Maybe that's why I was a social pariah," Sami mused. "I hadn't discovered Kat."

"You weren't a social pariah!" Cassie protested.

"Oh, come on. I was the nerdy student president. I wasn't getting invites to the tailgate parties."

"All it took was the apocalypse." Jimmy wrestled her down, and she squealed as he tickled her.

Kat sighed. "Just get into the kitchen, okay? We need to work out what we're doing from here on out."

She left them to their carry-on and found the downstairs powder room. Thanks to the farmhouse having its own well and septic system, they had flushing toilets. It was funny the things she'd once taken for granted could now make her so happy.

Running water was a luxury she'd never take for granted again; luckily her period had finished before they'd been kicked out of Sanford, obviously Chloe wasn't getting hers and Mackenzie and Rachel had both commented on how infrequently they were getting theirs.

Kat was a little sore, but in the most delicious way. Being with Quinn had been all-encompassing—it wasn't just sex, the intimacy they'd shared went beyond that.

Her feelings went *way* beyond that.

She'd never imagined she'd get her own happily ever after, especially not since the end of the world. But she was starting to believe him when he said his did, too.

A THIRD POT of coffee had been started and opinions were getting heated—they couldn't agree on anything; voices were raised, and no one was listening.

The kitchen was full and as Kat looked around at her found family her frustration rose. It was like none of them had learned anything.

They needed to work together.

"Stop," she said. When no one heard her, she pushed back her chair and stood up. "Guys, stop. This is insane. We won't work out anything if we keep talking over the top of each other."

It wasn't until Quinn stood, and then Cassie, that the voices died down.

"What? What are you doing?" Rachel asked.

"What are *you* doing?" Kat countered. "Rach, you're the best person to lead us, but you're not listening. No one is listening."

In the silence she sat back down. Quinn joined her, squeezing her hand.

"If you're going to keep ignoring what we have to say, then there's no point in us being here." Cassie put a hand on her hip as the other teenagers nodded.

"No offence, but you're still kids," Jesse said.

"Fuck this." Stephen slapped the table and stood. "When you're ready to hear what we have to say, you can come find us."

"Wait," Kat called after the teenagers. "Let's try this again."

They didn't return.

"Great." Kat blew out a heavy breath. She took a sip of her coffee and refocused her thoughts. "Let's take it in turns to give our opinion, and no one–" She looked at Rachel. "Can interrupt. And then we can have a civilized discussion based on what we hear. Agreed?"

Everyone nodded.

"Rach, you want to start?" Mackenzie asked.

"I'm pissed to have lost Sanford. Not only is it our best chance of survival, but it's our *home*," Rachel said. "I had plans on using our stores of whiskey to start trading with other communities, and I'd been talking with Maggie and Tabitha about expanding our community garden to actual crops in the Spring..." She paused. "But I'm not pissed enough to think it's a good idea to try to re-take it. We have to move on from Sanford."

Chloe, face red, drew in a forceful breath.

"It's James' turn." Jesse put a hand over Chloe's. "Wait for him, and then it's you."

"I'm worried about our friends we've left behind. I know Maggie will rally them, but Lucy took Asaad's death really badly." James cleared his throat. "That said, I agree going back to Sanford will only lead to trouble. I've always said we should find a farmhouse that's already set up for cropping and livestock. We could be self-sustaining and far enough away from the crazies. That gang of teenagers, what did they call themselves?"

"Panthers," Rachel supplied.

"I know they were only kids, but they were dangerous. And what about the Mallrats they mentioned? As well set up as this house is, it's too close to other people. We need to move out of Dutton."

"I agree, we have to leave here." Chloe was twisting her hands together, but her voice was clear and strong. "We *have* to go back to Sanford. You said it, Rach. Sanford is our home, and it's where Ash is coming back to. If I'm not there, he won't know where to look for me. We'll never find each other."

No one spoke.

"I'm not stupid, I know you think he's dead," Chloe burst out. "But I know he's not. I'd know if he was." Her fist rested over her heart. "I'd know."

Jake put his arm around his sister, squeezing her.

"My turn?" Jesse asked.

"Yeah, go ahead," Jake said.

"I don't think it's safe to stay in Dutton for too long, but it's a good base to use while we search for a farmhouse—I like James' idea. That said, we shouldn't abandon Sanford completely. Maybe we could set up some kind of system with Maggie, where we go back every couple of weeks to check in? That way we'd know how they were going, and also if anyone new had arrived."

"That could work." Quinn's eyes narrowed thoughtfully. "But we'd have to keep our own location a secret from them. We can't risk our security by letting anyone know where we are."

"It won't be enough!" Chloe's chair legs squeaked as she pushed back forcefully and stood. "Ash won't wait for us to check back in. If I'm not there, he'll leave to find me. You can all do what you like, but I'm going back to Sanford and I'll beg them to let me stay. Mrs. White has always been decent to me, I'll take my chances." Tossing her hair back, she left the room.

"What? Chlo!" Kat tried to rise to follow her, but Quinn put a hand on her arm.

"Give her some space," Jake said. "She's upset. She's going to need time to accept that Ash is really gone."

"She's had two months, and she still thinks he's coming back," Mackenzie said. "And finding out she's pregnant... that hasn't helped."

"Because she can't grieve with any certainty." Kat shrugged. "I'm going to find her. As long as we're all together, I don't care what we do. I'm putting my vote behind whatever Quinn suggests."

She ignored Rachel's raised eyebrow and left the room.

She found Chloe in one of the bedrooms, muttering to herself and stuffing things into a backpack she'd obviously found among the many supplies that were stockpiled here.

"Babe, what are you doing?" Kat sat down on the bed and drew her legs up, wrapping her arms around them and resting her chin on her knees.

"What does it look like?"

"How are you going to get back to Sanford? The Panthers have the snowmobiles, and you know how hard the bus was to drive in these conditions."

"It won't be so bad. At least if I stick to the track Jake already made, it'll be easier." Chloe looked up from her haphazard packing. "You can't stop me."

"Jake's not going to give you the keys to the bus," she said gently.

"You think this is the first time I'll have gotten something from my brother that he didn't want me to have?"

"Okay. So say you make it to Sanford, what if they won't let you in?"

"Then I'll set up base at the truck stop, and put out signs on the road."

"Putting up a sign with an arrow saying 'I'm in here' is a surefire way to bring trouble to your door, Chlo." She stretched out her legs and leant back on her hands. "Are you really prepared to give up a comfortable bed like this..." she wiggled her butt on the mattress, "not to mention my delightful company?"

Chloe stilled, her serious eyes boring into Kat's.

"You don't understand. I'm prepared to do *anything* to find my husband."

———

QUINN'S HEAD was pounding by the time they finally agreed to not agree.

Even after everyone had their say, they couldn't reach a consensus; the stalemate went round and round in circles until the only thing they *could* agree was that no one would go anywhere until a plan had been decided on.

"So we all promise not to leave or do anything until we've got a plan. Right?" Rachel said.

"You want us to pinky swear?" Quinn ground out. He

was tired of the constant negotiation and wanted to find Kat. *Needed* to find Kat.

The little brat was an itch in his blood that only her presence could soothe.

"Don't be an asshole, Q," James said. "We're all doing the best we can."

Quinn didn't want to spend the energy arguing with him. He'd much rather use that energy to turn his inappropriate thoughts into actions and pound into Kat's tight little pussy.

"Sure." He pushed himself to his feet. "I'm out of here."

"I'm going to make food, you want to stick around for that?" Mackenzie asked.

"Nope," he called over his shoulder. There was only one thing he wanted to be eating right now.

He called out to Kat as he jogged up the staircase, his heavy footfalls announcing his intent; he was going caveman on her ass and taking her back to bed for the rest of the afternoon, and for damn sure nothing was distracting him from his goal.

"Hey." She was sitting in the hallway with her back to a door.

"What are you doing?"

"Making sure Chloe doesn't do anything stupid."

"If I tell you I'm going to do something stupid, would you come and babysit me?" He smirked at her, not trying to hide his dirty desires.

Now that he'd had this woman, he didn't know if he'd ever get enough.

"Maybe..." She grinned up at him.

He bent and picked her up, hoisting her over his shoulder. She swatted at his ass, which just made him laugh and bite hers, making her squeal.

"That didn't hurt, and you know it." To emphasize his point, he smacked her again.

When he got to their room, he kicked the door shut behind them and lowered Kat until her legs were wrapped around his waist. Stepping into the closed door, he pressed her back against it, planting his feet wide so he had complete stability and control.

He was going to linger–lavish her with every ounce of the adoration she deserved.

She rested her head against the door, tilting her face to regard him. "Quinn Brent, are you going to ravish me?"

The cheeky glint in her eyes made him squeeze her harder.

"Don't be a brat," he growled.

"Make me," she challenged.

His lips captured hers, and she stopped her sass with a breathy gasp. Opening her mouth she accepted his intrusion, moaning a little as he slanted his lips over hers and plundered. He feasted, insatiable for her taste. Her tongue, sweet and hot, met his thrusts with a dizzying fervor–their lust feeding off of each other.

It was the kind of kiss that men went to war over.

She was lush perfection; her pussy grinding into him and her hands tangled in his hair. He tilted his head, demanding deeper access. He wanted to consume her.

When they finally broke apart, panting, he gripped her ass and lifted her up and down, rubbing her along the length of his cock until her eyes rolled back with the intensity of the friction.

"Oh, god. The seam of my jeans..."

"Getting you in just the right spot, huh, darlin'?"

"Keep going, don't stop," she begged, pouty lips parted. "I could... I'm going to..."

And she splintered apart in his arms, her orgasm washing away her strength until she was only upright because he was holding her pinned.

"Holy fuck," she breathed. "You just got me off in two point five seconds, and I've still got my clothes on."

"Let's fix that." He used one hand to unbutton the soft plaid flannel she was wearing, glimpsing creamy cleavage encased in black lace.

Christ, she might not be the only one coming in their pants.

When her shirt was gaping open, he nuzzled between her tits, pulling the lacy cups down so they sat beneath her plump breasts, pushing them up and exposing them to his hunger.

He licked across one sensitive nipple, captivated by the way it furled into an even tighter bud. Sucking it into the heat of his mouth he suckled, using the suction of his tongue to draw it further in, nipping gently when her thighs tightened around him.

He let go with a pop and immediately went to work on the other nipple, gorging himself on her sumptuous flesh and reveling in her yearning whimpers.

"Quinn, I need..." She wasn't gentle when she tugged on his hair to bring his face level with hers. "I need more."

She wasn't the only one. His balls were heavy and throbbing, and his cock was about to burst through his jeans. But he loved the foreplay–the tease of the slow burn.

Which was lucky, because being endowed with his cock meant if she wasn't turned on, there'd be no getting it on. So as wet as he knew Kat was right now, he wasn't even *nearly* finished with all the ways she was going to come before they actually had sex.

He whispered feather-light kisses down the slender

column of her neck, sinking his teeth in lightly when she squirmed.

"Quinn, please!"

"Darlin', I hope you're not asking for what I think you're asking for. Because I've told you before, we're taking this slow." He sucked at her soft skin, wanting to leave his claim.

In response, she began rubbing herself against him, clutching at the back of his neck.

She was such a brat.

"Right, that's it." He grabbed under her ass and spun, stalking to the bed and dumping her back onto it. Her perky tits bounced and her eyes flashed indignantly.

"You can't just throw me around!"

"Sure I can." He gripped the hem of his Henley and undershirt, removing them both in one swift movement and smirking as he caught her eyes roving over his bare chest.

When he snapped open his belt buckle and drew the leather through the loops to snap it between his hands, she licked her lower lip.

"You going to let me tie you up, darlin'?"

With her eyes locked on his, she brought her wrists together and slowly raised her arms.

This woman *slayed* him.

"Get undressed, first. I want to see every inch of your gorgeous body."

His throat was dry, and he swallowed, his eyes tracking every movement as she took off her clothes until she was gloriously naked, reclining on the bed like the queen she was.

"Get on your hands and knees, facing the head of the bed," he instructed, mesmerized by her peach of an ass as she complied.

"Like this?" She looked back over her shoulder at him,

provocative and full of so much sass he wanted to kiss her senseless all over again. Unable to help himself, he rubbed a hand over the front of his jeans, his erection straining for release.

"Put your hands up on the bed rail. I'm going to tie you there, and then you're going to ride my face until you're screaming my name."

She was panting by the time her hands were secured and her arousal was slick and dripping between her legs. With wordless urgency he climbed onto the bed and slid beneath her, easily rearranging her tiny body until she was straddling his face and *Jesus fucking Christ* she was a sensory overload. Her scent, her taste...

Placing his hands on her hips he buried his face in her pussy, opening his mouth and licking deep into her folds. She was shuddering and chanting his name as he sucked her clit and he urged her to rock against him with his hands.

Her movements were small and slow, until he buried his tongue into her tight entrance and then she was riding him, making small grunts of effort as she gyrated her hips and rocked, building a rhythm to his thrusting tongue.

He felt the moment her pussy fluttered and contracted, and then she was screaming her release, her thighs clamped violently around his head as she rode out the orgasm.

When she slowed and then stilled, her thighs were shaking, and she was sobbing and laughing. Taking one last lick, he lifted her and slid from beneath her, running a hand along her back and into the disheveled hair of her bowed head.

Sagging against her restraint, she turned her head to him, eyes dazed and mouth lax.

He reached out to cup her face, pushing his thumb

between her lips. When she sucked him in, his balls drew tight and his plans for slow and steady were shot to hell.

With a snap he had her wrists released and he caught her as she slumped forward, boneless with the release he'd wrung from her.

Moving back to sit against the headboard he dragged her onto his lap.

"Climb on, darlin'. We're not finished yet."

She obeyed without question, climbing up his chest to reach his face and kissing him with abandon. He opened his mouth for her and she sank into him, devouring her own taste.

Gasping, she pulled away, eyes feverish with lust.

"I need you, Quinn. Now."

He dislodged her long enough to shed his jeans and sheath a condom, and then she was back in his lap and rising on her knees to sink onto him, her thighs straining wide and her cunt dripping.

"Take it slow," he warned, holding the base of his cock as her tight warmth encased the tip. Gripping his shoulders she looked down, watching as she slid further onto him. It was the sweetest torture, and Quinn had to hold himself back from punching his hips upwards and impaling himself.

"You don't have to... go all the–" But she could and she did, and Quinn lost coherent thought as she settled over him, full to the hilt.

"Fuck-fuck-fuck." She sucked in a breath. "So deep. So good."

"You're okay?"

"Just let me... adjust."

They stayed that way, eyes locked and breathing heavily. Quinn had never felt this kind of deep connection in his life. "I love you."

"I know." And she was kissing him again and rocking, rocking. Her pussy was impossibly tight, clenching around him until he saw stars behind his eyelids.

"Kat. Darlin'. I need to fuck you now, okay?"

"Yes, please."

He held her hips steady in a bruising grip and fucked up into her, pumping his hips at a punishing pace that had her writing and then sobbing through another orgasm.

Grinding into her he pulled her closer, closer. Climaxing with a soft groan of desperation.

THEY RECOVERED IN SLOW DEGREES, trading soft kisses and murmured words. She was curled into his side and he rolled so he could spoon her, pulling her tighter and kissing her shoulder.

She fidgeted, her fingers worrying the corner of the sheet.

"What's wrong, darlin'?"

"Chloe." She sighed. "She's determined to get back to Sanford."

"That's a tomorrow problem. Sleep now."

DAY 67

Dawn had only just broken the horizon when Jim, Chris, Matt and Gunner arrived at the safehouse. Quinn heard the front door slam and rolled out of bed, still shrugging on a shirt as he descended the stairs.

"You've got a lot of nerve showing up here." His voice was low, his tone lethal.

"What's your problem?" Jim swung towards him, shrugging out of jacket.

"My problem is you."

Jake and Mackenzie rushed into the hallway from the kitchen, looking between Quinn and Jim warily.

"Look, I didn't know that Bronwyn was going to do what she did." Jim held up his hands, palms out. "That's not on me."

Something dark and dangerous rose in Quinn.

"No. What's on you is taking advantage of a teenage student." He was deceptively calm, but Jim wasn't a fool–he could sense the menace and he stilled.

"Whatever you think you know, you haven't heard my side of the story," Jim said.

"What is he talking about? We're fucking freezing, can we just come in and eat something?" Matt asked, bending to take off his boots and apparently oblivious to the mud and snow he'd already trekked inside.

"Yeah, yeah." Jim waved his men to the kitchen. "Jake, can you sort them some food? And get Rachel, I need her ASAP."

Quinn's upper lip curled. "I don't think you get it. You're not welcome here."

"Jesus Christ! Whatever the little slut told you, it isn't true."

Jim was on the floor, knocked out cold, before he'd even registered Quinn's lethal swing.

CHAPTER TEN

Kat stood at the top of the stairs as everyone argued whether to drag Jim's unconscious body onto the front porch, or into the kitchen.

She actually didn't care one way or the other. Because she didn't plan on being here when he came to. Being called a slut was a punch to the gut, and she had no interest in defending herself–to him, or anyone.

And his arrival was the distraction she needed.

She knew with complete certainty that Chloe wouldn't care about the agreement to stay put until a plan had been made. She was packed and ready, just waiting for her opportunity to get back to Sanford.

Last night, as she'd lain awake, Kat knew she had to do.

Pulling her beanie and gloves on, she slipped down the stairs as Jim was taken to the kitchen. Undetected, she snuck to the back door that led to the laundry room and then outside. Yesterday she'd spotted a crate of spray paints in the garage, which had sparked the idea for her plan.

Loading several into her backpack she crept out of the garage and around the side of the house. Checking the coast was clear, she ducked onto the front porch and approached the door, already shaking a can of paint.

In seconds, she'd made her mark:

Always Forever.

It was what Chloe and Ash had said to each other since they were love-struck teenagers; they would part with one saying 'always' and the other saying 'forever'. They even had it engraved on the inside of their wedding bands.

Snapping on a pair of snowshoes, Kat looked out at the empty street, glad the day was bright and windless. She knew what she was doing would have Rachel spitting mad, and she didn't want to think what Quinn would say.

But it had to be done.

Resolutely, she started down the block, stopping when she got to the corner. Her plan had been to spray the street sign, but she hadn't considered she wouldn't be tall enough to reach.

"Shit," she muttered.

"What are you doing?"

Shrieking, she whirled around. "Cass! You scared the shit out of me!"

"You know we're not meant to be out here, right?" Sami asked.

"So what are you doing here, then?" Kat put her hands on her hips, looking at the five teenagers who had apparently followed her.

"We asked you first," Stephen countered, his dimple popping in a cheeky grin.

Kat huffed. "Fine, if you're going to break the rules, you can help me."

"We're cool with breaking the rules, but why are we doing it?" said Lucas, looking from the can of paint and back to her.

"I'm making a trail from all major roads into Dutton, that lead here." Kat shook the spray can.

"And *why* are you doing that?" Jimmy tilted his head. "Doing stupid shit is fine, but that seems... extra stupid."

"Couldn't that lead those gangs right to us?" Cassie asked.

"Only if they know what to look for, and what it means. And they don't, and won't."

"And you know that, how?" Cassie looked at her skeptically. "What exactly are you painting?"

"You didn't see the front door?"

"We came out the back," Stephen said.

"I'm painting the words Always Forever. It's something that Ash will know to follow, and it will convince Chloe to stay. Otherwise, she's going back to Sanford to wait for him."

"And what if he doesn't come through Dutton?" Jimmy asked. "I was failing geography, but there's got to be a million different ways he could take to get home, and they wouldn't all be through Dutton."

"True, but we have to do something, otherwise Chloe's going to put herself in danger. And I'd much rather take that risk for her, and do this."

She pulled out a map, showing them the street corners she'd marked with the different routes Ash could possibly take, depending on which road he arrived on.

"Uh, that's a lot of signs," Cassie commented, scrunching up her nose as she considered the map.

"I didn't say I'd get it all done in one day. But it's a start. And now that I have help, we'll get twice as much done,"

Kat replied. "Now, who's giving me a boost to paint this sign?"

THEY WORKED INTO THE MORNING, with Kat looking over her shoulder expecting Quinn to have tracked her down already. It's not like they could be stealthy with the tracks they were leaving in the snow.

Her forefinger was sore from pressing down the spray nozzle, and her gloves were paint stained, but they'd created an efficient system working in two teams and had covered more ground than Kat could have done in a day working by herself.

She leaned against a building with the boys, as they waited for Sami and Cassie to signal from each end of the block that they were clear. When they waved, Kat and Stephen headed towards Cassie, and Jimmy and Lucas went to Sami.

The knees of Kat's jeans were wet from Stephen having dropped her a time or two in the snow, but alternating with Cassie to get on his shoulders sure beat carrying a ladder around with her.

"You think this is going to help Chloe? Like, give her some kind of closure?" Stephen asked, kicking at a snow-covered fire hydrant.

"I don't know. I hope so." Kat shook the can she was holding.

She tried not to think about the people they'd lost. It hurt too much. She'd been estranged from her mom, but Ash wasn't just Chloe's husband–he was Kat's friend, too.

"So you don't think he could still be alive?" Cassie said.

"I mean, maybe?" Kat sighed. "But it's been, what? Two months? The chances aren't great." She dug around in her coat pocket and withdrew two mini bottles of vodka, throwing one to Cassie. "You can share one."

"We really are breaking all the rules, huh?" Cassie grinned, uncapping the bottle and wincing when she took a sip and passed it to Stephen. "One way to keep warm out here."

Kat didn't answer, just slugged back her own bottle.

She knew she needed to cut back on the drinking, but she also didn't want to waste the alcohol. She may as well drink it, and then it would be gone and she could stop.

The burn down her throat was familiar and comforting, and she uncapped another bottle before she could think about it too closely.

The sooner they were gone, the sooner she'd get her abstinence on.

"Any more of those?" Lucas called out as the other three approached.

Kat tossed them each a bottle.

"Thanks." Lucas winked at her. "I wish the other adults were as cool as you. No one listens to us."

"Well, I know why they don't listen to you," Jimmy ribbed. "But the rest of us are more than capable of contributing to the discussion."

They continued walking along the route Kat had charted, stopping when they passed the smashed front windows of a liquor store.

"You think it's worth checking to see there's anything left inside?" Stephen asked, using the toe of his boot to nudge the broken door open.

"Not a chance. Joints like this would have been the first places looted," Jimmy responded.

"Guys..." Kat held up a hand, "do you hear that?"

She wasn't sure what had caught her attention, but something felt... off.

When she couldn't hold her breath any longer, she let it out in a rush. The teens looked at her, expectant.

"I don't hear anything," Cassie said, tilting her head.

"Maybe we should head back." Kat hoisted her backpack higher over her shoulders, looking both ways along the street. "You didn't bring any weapons with you, did you?"

Stephen huffed. "As if we'd be trusted to carry."

Kat pursed her lips, thinking. She'd considered bringing a gun, but she wasn't that confident in using them, and didn't want to waste the time to locate one before she left. And honestly, she'd only been planning on doing a block or two—just enough to make a start and show Chloe she had another option.

With the help of the teens, she'd strayed much further from the safehouse than she'd intended. She swallowed, a clammy heat washing over her.

They needed to get back. Now.

"What are your spidey senses telling you?" Lucas asked.

Kat shot him a look. She'd never felt less like joking.

"I don't think we're alone," she said quietly. "Get inside the liquor store. Now."

"The snow is clear of tracks, we'd see if—" Cassie broke off, wide eyes caught on movement in a store across the street.

"Go! Now!" Kat pushed Sami ahead of her and ran into the store, the others hot on her heels just as people exploded out of the buildings behind them.

"Don't stop! There should be a back door," she shouted, stopping to shepherd the teens ahead of her and looking over her shoulder to see at least ten armed people running towards them.

She stumbled into Jimmy's back, the back of the store was dark and they'd crowded against a boarded up door, frantically trying to pull off the boards nailed in.

"We're trapped!" Cassie yelled, spinning to Kat. "There's no way out."

Breath heaving, the teens looked to her, fear making their faces look years younger.

"Okay. Okay." Kat gulped, heart racing and adrenaline spiked. She turned to face the front of the store.

Whoever was outside, they'd stopped on the pavement.

"Maybe... I mean, they could be friendly?" Sami said, huddled into Jimmy's side.

"Not with that kind of welcome, they're not," Stephen muttered.

"Come out, come out, wherever you are," sing-songed a female voice. "Actually, that's not right, we know exactly where you are."

"We're not a threat," Kat called back. "We can just leave, and you'll never see us again."

"Come out and talk with us. I'll even get my boys to put their guns away."

"She's just a girl!" Sami said, straightening. "They're kids, like us."

Kat didn't care how old they were. They were armed and had the advantage. Not to mention this was obviously a tactical move–they'd cornered their prey like animals.

And Kat didn't like feeling like prey.

"You sure we can't get through that door?" she asked Stephen, not taking her eyes off the small blonde figure standing out the front.

"Not without tools," Stephen replied.

"It would be rude not to come out, when I've asked so nicely," Blondie called.

"You stay here, I'll talk to her." Kat pulled her shoulders back. She could do this. She'd gotten them into this mess, and she was going to get them out.

"No way. We stand together." Lucas came up beside her.

Cautiously, they all approached the front, squinting at the backlit figures fanned out before them. Contrary to what Blondie had promised, their weapons were still out but weren't pointed at them.

Kat's hands were sweating in her gloves, and her mouth was dry as they stepped outside.

This was bad.

"Ah, there you are. The mother duck with all her ducklings. Kat, isn't it?" Blondie took a step forward and Kat's stomach dropped. They'd been stalking them for long enough to hear their conversation and pick up their names.

"Now, we already know you're not carrying anything we need. Unless you've got more of that alcohol in your pack?" Blondie arched a perfectly sculpted eyebrow.

"You can have everything." Kat shrugged off her backpack and threw it forward to land at the girl's feet.

"Mmmm. I'm more interested in where you've come from." Blondie flashed white teeth.

"We can't tell you that," Kat replied tightly.

"I thought you might say that. Billy?" Blondie gestured to one of the hulking boys beside her and the kid raised his shotgun, a crazed glint to his eyes.

"I know you!" Lucas burst out. "You're the quarterback for the Sacred Heart High football team. I played against you last year."

"Then you probably lost." Billy smirked.

"The Panthers," Kat breathed.

"Yeah, that's the name of your team. The Panthers," Lucas said.

"Well done." Blondie clapped condescendingly. "But that was the old world, and this is the new. And you're in our territory. So you're going to need to tell us where you've come from."

"We don't have a base," Kat said. "We're from Sanford, but we're just travelling through."

"Wrong." Blondie smiled sadly. "We heard you talking. There are more of you in a safehouse."

"Missy, I told you we should just follow their tracks back," said a well-built blonde kid who looked a lot like her. Brother, maybe?

"And I told you, Sean, that I wanted to see how truthful these good people could be." Missy smiled at Kat. "Didn't your parents teach you it was wrong to lie?"

"Fuck this!" Lucas threw out his hands. "What are you gonna do? Shoot us?"

Missy narrowed her eyes and, without taking her gaze from Lucas, lifted a finger.

A shot fired, splintering savagely through Kat's eardrums. Her hands rose to cover her ears and Lucas fell to the ground at her feet, the snow turning red around him.

"No!" Kat screamed, dropping to her knees and falling over his lifeless body. Shouts and screams were echoing in her head, but all she could see were Lucas' sightless eyes. She passed a trembling hand over them, closing the eyelids.

Time took on a hazy quality. Surreal and sluggish. Kat looked at her hands, at the bright red blood that streaked her skin. When had she taken off her gloves?

"Kat. Kat!" Cassie was yelling at her.

She looked up just as Jimmy lunged at Missy. "You bitch!"

And then another gunshot cracked, and Jimmy was falling, a surprised look on his face. Red bloomed across his chest as he hit the snow, his mouth open in a silent scream.

Sami's anguished scream tore through Kat, forcing her to her feet. "Stop, stop! I'll tell you where the safehouse is," she cried.

"Missy, Chuck's on the radio. Something's going down..." One of the boys held a radio handset, his face grim. "I didn't catch that, repeat. Over."

"Troy, tell Chuck—" Missy stopped, cut off by the crackle of the radio. "What was that? What did Chuck say?"

"Fuck! It's the Mallrats! We need to go!" Panic lit up Troy as he looked to Missy.

"They have seriously bad timing," Missy snapped, irritation flashing across her face.

"What did you do?" Sami screamed, bending over Jimmy and pressing her hands to the brutal wound, futilely trying to stop the gush of blood. "You've killed him!" She lurched to her feet, hands dripping and face murderous.

Distracted, Missy glanced at Sami dismissively and then back to Troy.

"I will hunt you down, you bitch. I will—" A third gunshot rent the air, and Sami pin-wheeled her arms as she fell backward, a small neat hole marring her forehead.

"Loyalty doesn't go unpunished," Missy said, pocketing her handgun. "Come on boys, let's move out."

———

A VICIOUS BRUISE had spread across Jim's face during the hour or two they'd debated in the kitchen. He was sticking by his story that he'd had nothing to do with Bronwyn's actions, and swore he would discipline them when he returned.

"I'm telling you, come back with me and we'll make it right." Jim's voice was ragged, having talked at them relentlessly.

"Even if you could do that, I want nothing to do with you." Quinn stared the other man down. "There is no excuse for what you did to Kat."

She was the only reason Quinn wasn't tearing this man apart. By some miracle Kat was still asleep upstairs, and the bloodbath he was itching to inflict would wake her.

"I've explained–"

"Stop right there." Rachel cut Jim off. "If you say one more word against her, I'll let Quinn cut your tongue out."

"She's the reason his daughter is missing," Gunner pointed out, raising his hands defensively when all heads swung his way. "What? I'm just saying."

"Shut your face, or you'll be next," Mackenzie snapped.

Chris and Matt exchanged a look, and Quinn double-checked their weapons were still leaning against the wall behind him and out of their reach.

"Fine, fine," Jim blustered. "You don't have to come back to Sanford. But Rachel, we need you. You have to come with us."

"She doesn't have to do a goddamn thing you say!" James slammed his fist down on the table. "Is anyone else sick of listening to this guy? I say we kick them out and say good riddance."

"You don't understand." Jim's demeanour turned desperate, his head shaking as sweat broke out across his brow. "Caroline radioed and Archer is sick."

"And your son being sick is my problem, how?" Rachel crossed her arms across her chest.

"You're the closest thing we have to a doctor. I know you're only a vet but–"

"*Only* a vet?" Rachel barked a humorless laugh. "You know doctors study to work with one species, and I have a doctorate to work with multiple species, right?"

"Exactly! That's why we need you!" Jim's eyes were overly bright. "You have to come back with us."

"What's wrong with Archer?" Rachel asked, arms still crossed.

"Not a chance!" James pushed back from the table and stood. "You're not going with them." Rachel shot him a glance, and he sat back down, fists clenched.

She looked expectantly at Jim. "Well?"

"He has a fever, Caro says he's burning up."

"So dose him up on Tylenol. There are antibiotics in the warehouse, use those if he needs them."

"But how will we know if he needs them?"

"Figure it out. That's not my problem," Rachel snapped. "You know what *is* my problem? Working out where we're going to live, because *your* wife let us be kicked out of our home."

"I'm done with this." Quinn's patience snapped. "Your time is up. We've fed you, and you've got enough gas to get back to Sanford. Get the fuck out of my sight, before you've got more than a bruised face."

When Matt stood and reached for his rifle, Quinn blocked him. "Yeah, you're not taking that."

"You can't let us go out there without weapons," Chris protested, coming to stand beside Matt.

Quinn growled, and both men stepped back.

The violence that heated Quinn's blood wanted them to object. Wanted the opportunity to unleash the fury that had been building ever since Kat had revealed her secret.

"We're going." Jim stood, a righteous anger reinvigorating him. "But don't come crawling back to beg for our help, because that door has closed. You're no longer welcome in Sanford."

"That's old news," Jake scoffed, putting his arm around a quietly seething Mackenzie. "Q, you gonna help me see these gentlemen out?"

"My pleasure." Quinn picked up Chris and Matt's rifles, passing one to Jake as Rachel took possession of the third and fourth one. It was a nice feeling, removing these men with their own guns.

"You're going to regret this," Jim warned, as the four men stepped off the front porch and got onto their snowmobiles.

"Nope, don't think we will," Rachel shot back, giving him the finger.

Quinn watched them roar off, knowing his only regret was not inflicting more damage on the man who had damaged a young and vulnerable girl.

"Where is Kat?" Rachel asked, as though only just realizing she wasn't present.

"Still asleep," Quinn replied, turning to go back inside.

"Still? That girl never sleeps in—she's an early riser."

True. Kat was annoyingly perky in the morning. Quinn frowned.

Maybe she was just hiding out upstairs because she didn't want to face Jim?

The crack of a gunshot in the distance startled them into silence.

"What was that?" Jake looked between Rachel and Quinn.

"Gunshot," said Quinn, an icy feeling trickling down

his spine. He didn't like the fact he hadn't seen Kat in a couple of hours.

"You think it's the Panthers?" asked Jake.

"Or the Mallrats, whoever they are." Rachel opened the front door, only to stop when they heard another shot, and then another just seconds later. "I hate that we're so close to these gangs. We need to get away from Dutton."

"Guys, have you seen Kat?" Jesse was coming down the stairs. "Jesus, close the door! You're letting all our heat out."

Quinn shut the door behind Rachel and Jake, and looked up at Jesse. "What do you mean? Isn't she upstairs?"

"Maybe she's with Chloe?" Rachel suggested. "Chlo wasn't feeling well and went upstairs to rest."

"She's not with me." Chloe came to stand beside Jesse, biting her lip. "She's done something stupid, I know it."

"What kind of stupid?" Quinn took the stairs two at a time and then ran to the bedroom he shared with Kat. He half expected her rumpled head to lift from the pillows, smiling sleepily at him.

But he already knew in his gut she wasn't here.

"Chloe?" He called, spinning from the doorway. "What kind of stupid?"

Chloe fidgeted with her hands. "She said she'd come up with an option that didn't involve me going back to Sanford. I don't know what she was thinking, but she seemed pretty determined."

"Shit. Shit!" Quinn slammed his fist into the wall, not caring about the hole it left in the drywall. Where the hell had she gone, and what was she doing?

"Did she talk to Mac or Rachel?" He was already striding for the stairs, calling their names as he descended.

"What? Jesus, what's the emergency?" Rachel called back from the kitchen.

"It's Kat. She's gone." Quinn's throat closed over the words, his chest tight.

Why didn't she trust him enough to let him help her?

"She's upstairs." Mackenzie was stirring something on the stove.

"She's not! Chloe said something about her making some kind of plan, did she talk to either of you about it?" Quinn's knuckles whitened as he clenched the back of the kitchen chair. An urgency had gripped him, and he needed to find her *now*. "Do you have any idea what she might be doing?"

"She didn't stick around for our discussion yesterday. Didn't she say she was happy to do whatever you wanted?" Rachel shrugged. "She won't have gone far. It's too cold, and Dutton's too dangerous to go roaming about."

"She thinks she's helping Chloe," Quinn grit out.

"Oh." Mackenzie turned from the stove, face white. "Then I wouldn't put anything past her."

IT TOOK minutes for Quinn to get his outdoor clothes on and grab his Ruger and a rifle.

"Did you say you had extra ammo for the Ruger in your stores here?" he called to Jake, taking the water bottle Mackenzie passed him.

"Already got it." Jake gave him a box, which Quinn stuffed into his backpack.

"I've got extra for the rifles, too," said Jesse, coming to stand beside him holding a rifle and wearing his bulky jacket.

"What are you doing?" Quinn shouldered his pack, looking at Jesse.

"Coming with you." Jesse shrugged. "Whatever she's doing, she's doing it for Chloe. So if she needs help, I'm in."

Quinn wasn't going to waste time arguing. In fact, he'd be glad for the company. "Let's roll out. One good thing about the snow, we should be able to find and follow her track easily enough."

Mackenzie and Rachel followed them onto the front porch, their arms around a sobbing Chloe. "She's going to be fine," Mackenzie said. Whether she was trying to reassure Chloe or herself, Quinn couldn't be sure.

He and Jesse strode out onto the street, awkward on snowshoes they hadn't used before.

"This is harder than it looks," Jesse muttered.

"Is that..." Quinn shaded his eyes, looking down the street. "It's Stephen and Cassie." Lead settled in his gut. "And something's wrong."

The teenagers were stumbling, arms around each other as they made their way toward the safehouse. Quinn froze, watching them advance. The closer they got, the clearer their distress became.

"What the hell happened to them?" Jesse said in a low voice. "Rach? We need you out here," he called over his shoulder.

The girls ran onto the street, engulfing the teenagers as they reached them. Quinn looked back in the direction they'd come from. Where was Kat?

Stephen and Cassie appeared to be in shock, neither able to answer the questions thrown at them. Tears streamed down Cassie's face and Stephen couldn't meet anyone's eyes.

"Get them inside," Rachel instructed. She turned to Quinn. "I don't think you should leave yet. We need to know what's happened."

Quinn nodded curtly, acutely aware of the dark blood stains streaking both the teens.

"Where is Kat? Is she with you?" He grabbed at Stephen's shoulder as he passed. The teen looked back with a blank expression.

Fuck. This was bad.

"She said she couldn't come back." Cassie had stopped walking, and was staring at Quinn with devastation carved into her face. "It's her fault they're dead."

CHAPTER ELEVEN

DAY 68

Kat was spiraling, and she didn't care. She *deserved* to spiral, to descend into the viscous despair that was sucking her under.

She was curled up in an armchair in a furniture store, not exactly sure how she'd made it there. When she'd walked away from Cassie and Stephen, she just knew she had to disappear.

It was bright daylight now, and she supposed it was the next morning. Time had no meaning.

Registering the buttery soft leather beneath her, she jerked upright. She had no right to be comfortable and being so triggered a sour self-loathing she couldn't shake, no matter how many times she swallowed.

Standing, she shook at the pins and needles in her legs and then allowed herself to crumple onto the floor. It was cold and unyielding, and she welcomed the discomfort. It was a distraction from the memory of Lucas' dead eyes. Of

Sami's lifeless body and the red-stained snow that surrounded Jimmy's body.

It was her selfishness–her impulsiveness–that had led them into that situation. And they hadn't walked away from it.

Three dead kids.

And it was Kat's fault.

She swiped angrily at the tears that wouldn't stop. She had no right to grieve their deaths. Not when it was because of her they were no longer living. Breathing. Laughing. Loving.

They were no longer.

Minutes turned into hours as she allowed the guilt to pick away at her, eroding her sense of self-worth and destroying any self-preservation instincts that tried to surface. She didn't deserve to eat, to drink, to sleep. She would waste away here, in this furniture store, and no one would come to pick up the pieces. Not this time.

No one was coming for her, and she couldn't face them if they did.

At some point she started pacing the store, Sami's sweet smile dogging her every step.

She'd killed them, and then abandoned Cassie and Stephen.

She stilled, horrified. She'd left them.

Without a second thought she headed to the store's entrance, pushing open the glass door and walking outside. The cold didn't register. She briefly considered the threat of Panthers or Mallrats and then dismissed them. Who cared if they came for her?

But she had to know that Cassie and Stephen made it back to the safehouse.

It took several blocks of aimless wandering–hands

burning in the cold because she'd lost her gloves–until Kat realized she had no idea where she was. The map was no longer in her pocket and none of the streets looked familiar.

She was lost.

The sun was dipping below the skyline, and the wind had picked up. She couldn't stop shivering and back-tracking to find the furniture store had been a failure.

She stumbled in the snow, finally leaning against the side of a building with her head bowed. An image of Quinn flashed through her mind and the longing was so strong she flinched. He would never look at her the same again.

She had lost him before she'd ever truly had him.

She registered the sound of an engine rumbling closer, but didn't bother to lift her head. She would get down on her knees for Missy and beg for oblivion.

She finally straightened when strong headlights washed over her, illuminating just how far darkness had fallen.

"Are you armed?" A male voice called over a speaker.

It was a military-type truck, with a covered-in back and men in the cab. Behind them was a jeep, with more men in uniform.

Kat wanted to laugh. The Army.

They were about two months too late.

She didn't bother to respond, just turned away. She was beyond saving.

"What are you doing out here alone?" The man had exited the truck and was walking towards her, snow crunching under his heavy black boots. She didn't raise her head, just stared at his boots as he came to stand before her.

"Jesus, I think she's loopy," he called back to the truck.

"Bring her in anyway."

It wasn't until strong arms locked around her that Kat

understood she actually did give a fuck, and she absolutely did not want to go with this man.

"No. Let go." She tried to shake him off. "I don't want to go with you."

"Well, that's too bad, little lady. Because we have orders to bring in all civilians."

He began forcing her to the waiting truck, supporting her weight when she refused to cooperate.

"You don't understand," she cried, trying to pry his fingers from their tight grip. "I don't need your help."

"Do you need assistance, Andy?" A man from the jeep came forward, his hands in his pockets and a swagger to his step.

"Nah, I've got my taser."

A shooting, excruciating pain radiated through Kat's side and her eyes rolled back in her head as every muscle in her body froze and she slumped into Andy's arms. The intensity of the pain blackened her vision and her skin felt like she was being stung by a thousand bees.

When comprehension returned, she was being thrown into the back of the truck; the impact jarring her hip bone and her head hitting someone's knee.

She cried out, but whoever she'd landed on remained silent apart from a soft grunt. Getting to her feet she looked around, seeing the bed of the truck was packed with people–men, women and children of all ages.

No one spoke.

When the truck started forward, Kat lurched off balance and fell against the same person, a woman who helped her back upright.

"Just sit down and be quiet," the woman said.

Kat shifted awkwardly, pain spearing her hip, until she was sitting against the wall of the truck with her knees bent before her. She shrugged her arms into her jacket so she could put her hands beneath her armpits; her fingers were numb and not functioning properly.

"I'm Kat."

"Brenda."

"What's going on?" she asked Brenda.

"They're taking us to the Colony."

"Colony?"

"You haven't heard of it? It's what's left of Chicago."

Kat's head was spinning. Back at Sanford they'd had shifts to monitor the ham radio around the clock. Apart from a group in New York City, they had found no other sizable groups. None that were on the airwaves, anyway.

How had they missed this?

"Where are you all from?" Kat asked. The headlights of the jeep behind them illuminated the truck well enough for her to see the exhausted faces surrounding her, even if no one would catch her eye.

"Most of us are from Greenville." Brenda sighed, stretching out her legs. "A couple got picked up on the highway on the way here. There's more still alive than I thought, that's for sure."

"I don't want to go to the Colony, I need to get off this truck." The back of the truck was open, and Kat could see the rushing blur of tarmac below them. A hot panic burned through her the further they drove. She would jump out and make a run for it when they slowed next.

The shock-induced shame she'd been drowning in had receded, replaced by an anxious alertness that expanded each mile this truck took her from her friends.

She could handle their anger, their disappointment and their disgust. But she couldn't handle being separated from them.

"Don't even think about it," Brenda warned, putting her age-spotted hand on Kat's knee. "That man over there jumped, and he survived the fall. But I don't know if he'll survive what they did to him." She glanced at a crumpled heap in the back corner, which Kat hadn't even realized was human.

"How is the military allowed to do this? Why are they taking people against their will?" Kat couldn't understand how this was happening.

"They're not real military," Brenda spat. "Sure, they're wearing the uniform and carrying the guns, but most of them are just regular people who've been recruited to fill the role. My son was a Marine, and no way would he have let this happen."

"They call themselves Guardians," the man sitting opposite Kat spoke up. "And they're taking us because they need us. Who else is going to rebuild?"

"Rebuild Chicago?" Kat furrowed her brow.

"Rebuild civilization, honey. This is the new world order, and we're the worker bees," the man replied wearily.

"And the breeders." A woman who looked to be Kat's age shuffled and crawled until she sat between Kat and the open back. "Hey, I'm Kelly. And I'd rather take my chances jumping."

Bile rose in Kat's throat and she swallowed convulsively. *Breeders?*

"You all need to shut your mouths," someone growled from further back in the track. "We're lucky they found us. Living in the Colony is better than scavenging to stay alive out here."

"How do you know that? You haven't been there," Brenda said. "And yeah, maybe it will be better. But these men who've picked us up sure aren't giving off a welcoming vibe."

Kat was only half listening, concentrating instead on watching to see if she recognized any landmarks they passed. When she escaped, she wanted to know how to get back.

She'd just spotted a Walmart when the truck slowed and pulled into the enormous outdoor parking lot. It was essentially empty, with only a few snow-covered mounds that must have been vehicles. Kat would have expected the place to be packed with deserted cars, but she guessed if people were well enough to have come here for supplies, then they were well enough to leave, too.

There wasn't a lot of cover for her to use, but if she was fast enough, she could make it to one of the mounds without being seen.

"I'm jumping," she whispered to Kelly. "You coming?"

"I'm already gone." Kelly flashed her teeth at Kat and leapt out into the snow, falling in a crouch and rolling into the snow out of sight.

The truck shuddered to a stop and Kat panicked–the window of time to jump was almost gone. Taking a deep breath, she bunched her muscles, hoping like hell this wouldn't hurt.

The headlights of the jeep swung wide as it pulled alongside the truck and she took advantage of the sudden darkness, springing from the truck and landing hard in the snow, not nearly as graceful as Kelly had.

Her knees jolted and the screaming pain in her hip caused her to gasp out loud. She scrambled for the cover of the snow mound, every second expecting the shock of a taser between her shoulder blades.

Collapsing behind the mound she tried desperately to

control her breathing, struggling to hear over her own panting. She didn't know what the soldiers were doing, or why they'd stopped, but their engines were still idling and no one had gotten out.

She glanced behind her, deliberating. It was a clear run to the front doors of the supercenter and if she kept low, she should stay out of sight.

"Kelly!" She whisper-shouted, straining her eyes in the darkness but unable to detect any movement. The other woman had run and not looked back.

Kat needed to do the same.

Ignoring her throbbing and exhausted body, she crouched and took off in a shuffle-run through the snow, pushing her aching thighs to lift higher, pump harder.

She'd expected the doors to be busted open, like pretty much every other retail store she'd seen in Dutton. But as she approached, her heart sank. They were sealed closed–thick-looking glass with a security screen rolled down behind it.

She was so close to safety, but still so far.

A sob caught in her throat and she heard the engines to the truck and the jeep turn off, voices ringing through the night air as the soldiers disembarked.

Fuck. Fuck!

She could barely see as she ran for the far corner of the building, trailing a hand along the wall–breathless and hobbling. She skirted an abandoned shopping cart, thankful the snow was less built-up and only ankle-deep, and finally reached the edge of the building, flinging herself around the corner and out of sight.

She could no longer see the lights from the vehicles or hear the soldiers. She was in complete darkness. Alone. And very much afraid.

———

HOW DO you find someone who doesn't want to be found?

Quinn and Jesse had followed the tracks to the liquor store where they'd stood in silence, grieving the loss of three of their own. Without a word, they had carried the bodies of the teenagers into the liquor store, arranging them carefully and pulling their jackets over their faces.

They would come back to bring them home.

But first, Kat.

It was impossible to find her tracks. It looked like after the Panthers had left, a pack of dogs had come through, and between the paw prints and the multiple sets of footprints, the ground was a mess.

Many of the tracks led into buildings, and from there... disappeared.

"We need to think like Kat," Quinn said thoughtfully. "Where would she have gone?"

"Who knows? That girl is chaos personified." Jesse looked down at the street map he was following. "She likes makeup, right? There's a Sephora at the end of this block."

"She's destroyed by guilt right now, not shopping." Quinn shot his friend a dark look. Why did no one take her seriously?

Yes, Kat was a walking hurricane—she was terrified of standing still, of being boring. She was flawed, but weren't they all? She was charming and spirited and loyal, with an enormous heart and endless capacity for compassion.

She was Kat.

And he would tear this town apart to find her.

. . .

THEY HAD SEARCHED through the night, only stopping in the early hours of the morning to sleep. With the rising of the sun they spotted another of Kat's 'Forever Always' signs and Quinn cursed, realizing they'd circled back to a street they had already walked.

"Q, we've been at this for hours. She could be anywhere." Jesse's shoulders were drooping and his feet dragged. "Let's head back to the safehouse, regroup and—"

"Go. I didn't ask you to come." There was no anger in Quinn. He truly appreciated Jesse's efforts. But for him? Until he found Kat, he wouldn't stop.

She was hurting and alone and his gut curdled thinking of the many things that could befall her out here. He and Jesse had been wary of running across the Panthers or the Mallrats; keeping their movements furtive and their voices low.

The thought of either of those gangs coming across Kat...

He grit his jaw and kept walking.

"At least let's have a break," Jesse called after him. "Hey, check out the sofas in that waiting area." He pointed to an open-plan office they could see through large glass windows.

Quinn took another step and then paused, slowly turning. He was thirsty, and eating something would boost his energy.

"Yeah, okay." He grimaced. "But only ten minutes."

Quinn readied himself to kick in the glass door, rolling his eyes when Jesse calmly tried the latch and it opened easily. The air inside was old, unpleasant in the same way flat soda was drinkable, but mildly disgusting.

Jesse sneezed and then sank onto one of the emerald green velvet sofas. "We should have slept on these. More comfortable than the floor of that other office." He closed his eyes. "Industrial carpeting should be illegal, I swear I've got a rash on my cheek from sleeping on it."

"Shut up and eat something."

Quinn didn't allow himself to sit on the matching sofa. He stood by the door and watched the street, uncapping his water bottle and eating a protein bar.

"Hey." Jesse popped open an eye. "What's that..."

"Shit. Shit! There's a truck coming this way!" Quinn hastily backed into the office space, ducking behind the reception counter. "Jesse! Get the fuck away from the windows!"

Jesse leapt to his feet, almost tripping over as he ran for cover. Just as he ducked behind the counter, a camo-painted truck rumbled past.

"That's military," Quinn muttered.

"And it's slowing down."

They watched, apprehension rising, as the truck rolled to a stop. Moments later an Army jeep pulled up behind, directly in front of the office.

"You think they're the same ones who were gathering up people in Arlington?" Jesse asked.

"Don't know. Don't want to find out."

"So we're not going to introduce ourselves?"

"Hell no." Quinn scowled at Jesse. "There is nothing good about what they're doing."

"Mike said most of the residents went with them willingly."

"Yeah, and they still took the unwilling ones."

A big guy with no neck and a swagger got out of the jeep and went to the driver's window of the truck. Movement caught Quinn's attention and his eyes widened when he saw the truck was packed with people.

Suddenly, a skinny guy jumped from the open back, making a run for it. He didn't get more than ten steps before several soldiers were upon him, knocking him to the ground and kicking into his prone form.

"Jesus!" Quinn spat, his fists clenching.

"They'll kill him if they don't stop." Jesse half rose into a crouch before Quinn pulled him back down.

The skinny guy, broken and bloody, was thrown back into the truck.

The protein bar Quinn had eaten sat heavy in his stomach as they waited for the vehicles to leave.

Waited. And waited.

"What the fuck are they doing?" Quinn's legs were cramping, and he needed a piss. The soldiers in the jeep were smoking and talking smack, and the whoever was driving the truck had yet to show themselves. "It's been what? An hour?"

"Closer to two."

"Fuck this, we're wasting time. Let's check out the back exit."

Bulky with their backpacks and rifles, they commando crawled from desk to desk, making their way to the back of the large room.

"Keep watch," Quinn said. "I'm going to find the restroom and then check for a back door."

Jesse nodded and settled himself behind two partition screens, using the small gap between them to monitor the front.

The restroom was easy to find. A way out, less so.

The back door had some kind of fancy electronic keypad, and it was built to withstand any force Quinn could throw at it. He had a broken chair to prove it.

Without electricity, they weren't getting out that way.

He lowered himself onto the floor next to Jesse and shook his head.

"The front door is our only option. We're stuck here."

Taking it in turns to keep watch, they dozed, making the most of the forced downtime. Two hours slipped into three, and then four.

"It'll be dark soon." Quinn tucked the map back into his jacket, having marked the areas they'd already searched and plotted their next move.

If these damn soldiers ever moved on.

"Let's move back up to the reception counter," Jesse suggested. "I want a better view of what they're doing."

"Freezing their balls off, that's what," Quinn grumbled, but he followed Jesse.

They stilled at the sound of the truck's ignition turning over, and then catching, roaring to life. Quinn closed his eyes in relief. *Finally.*

They watched as the soldiers moved out, cautiously approaching the front door as the jeep neared the corner of the block. Instead of picking up speed, the vehicles slowed and then stopped. Again.

"What the *fuck*?" Quinn slapped at the doorframe, frustration riding him hard.

"There's someone out there." Jesse squinted. "Is that? That's not..."

"It's Kat!" Quinn had unslung his rifle and was charging outside before Jesse could finish his sentence.

"Q. Quinn!"

And then Quinn was slammed into the snow from behind, Jesse on his back.

"Don't be a fucking idiot!" Jesse snapped. "You go charging over there and you'll end up in the truck, too."

"Get off me," Quinn growled. She was so close.

His whole body stiffened as Kat's body slumped, an anguished groan tearing through him when the guy with the swagger threw her into the truck.

"Quinn, listen to me." Jesse shook him hard. "We're two men, with two rifles. We storm them now and we're dead. You want to rescue Kat? We need to be smart. Take the time to think it through, and do it right."

The red brake lights went off, and both vehicles continued on.

Quinn struggled to find his feet in the snow with Jesse's entire weight pushing him down. He bellowed, shaking the other man loose, chest heaving and tears sliding into his beard.

"We'll follow them." Jesse stood up and readjusted his backpack. "We can't lose them, not with their tire tracks in the snow. We'll find out where they're taking her and get her back."

Every second they stood there deliberating, Kat got further away.

"We need a vehicle." Quinn looked around wildly. "Look for a four-wheel drive."

"Everything's covered in snow."

Quinn ignored him as he began running along the street. The parked vehicles were literally mounds of snow, and he was searching for an SUV-sized one.

"You're not serious?" Jesse puffed alongside him. "Even if we can dig it out, the battery is probably dead, or frozen. Or something."

"You're the pharmacist, I'm the mechanic." Quinn didn't spare him a glance. "So shut the fuck up and help me look."

. . .

IT TOOK them most of the night. Quinn's increasing desperation was making it hard to think straight. They'd eventually abandoned the idea of digging out a vehicle, and instead run along endless blocks to reach a residential area of Dutton.

The first garages they'd broken into were empty or only had smaller cars, but in the fifth one they found an older model four-wheel drive. They wasted more time swapping over to the snow tires that were stacked in the corner.

Turning the heat on full blast, he drove them back to where they'd last seen the soldiers. The underside of the vehicle only just cleared the height of the snow, and breaking trail in deep snow meant Quinn had to take it slower than he'd have liked.

He lost traction in some icy spots, having to adjust gears and zig-zag through the slushier areas, but it got easier when they picked up the soldiers' tracks. Like Jesse had said, their trail was easy to follow.

"They're hours ahead of us," Quinn growled, rolling his shoulders to find some relief from the tightness that gripped him.

"You want me to drive for a bit?"

"No." Quinn would go crazy, sitting in the passenger seat. At least if he was driving, he was doing something.

He drove on as the sky lightened into another day.

"The tracks turn here..."

"Stop! That's them there, at the Walmart!" Jesse leaned forward, peering through the windscreen. "Do you think they've seen us?"

They both reached for their rifles, ready to fire, but it didn't appear they'd been noticed. From half a block away, they watched as soldiers moved around, looking like they were readying to leave.

"Why are they here? I thought it would take us hours to catch them up." Quinn trained the scope of his rifle on the truck, frantic to catch sight of Kat. "It looks like they've spent the night."

"Why? We're not that far from Chicago. And where did they sleep? The Walmart?" Jesse yawned.

"We should get out and get closer. I want to hear what they're saying." Quinn was already reaching for his jacket, shrugging into it as he opened the door and climbed out.

A row of Goodwill donation bins along the side of the parking lot made the perfect cover, allowing them close enough to hear the soldiers.

"... we got a whole family last trip. This is the first time there's been no one here." A guy with a thick Italian accent ashed his cigarette. "I told the boss that Walmart isn't enough of a lure anymore. It's been too picked over."

"Whatever." A bald man shrugged. "It's a good thing. If we dismantle the trap, then we'll be able to actually sleep in there, instead of out here."

"Or we won't have to stop here at all. Spending the night here is bullshit."

The two dropped the butts of their cigarettes and walked away.

"Those assholes are trapping people!" Jesse whispered, outrage coloring his face.

"They don't act like they're military." Quinn observed the sloppy movements of the men–the way there didn't seem to be any kind of hierarchy.

"I haven't seen Kat." Jesse lowered his rifle, only to swing the scope back up. "What are they... oh. That's the skinny guy they beat up yesterday."

Two soldiers were lifting a body from the back of the truck, dumping it in the snow.

The truck started up, and the men jumped into the jeep.

"We need to get back to the four-wheel drive!" Quinn wanted to scream–to rent the heavens open with the depth of his desolation.

Kat was *so close.*

"We can't risk being seen. Wait," Jesse said. "We won't lose them."

When the soldiers were out of sight, Quinn and Jesse walked to where they'd camped overnight. The man they'd left behind was dead.

"Fucking assholes!" Jesse spat, kicking at the snow.

"And they've got Kat. Come on, let's go."

"Q, think about this. We're exhausted, and we're out-manned. The others are going to be worried because we've been gone so long."

"What are you saying? You want to turn around?" Quinn threw his arms in the air. "We're *so close!*"

"But we can't do anything! We need more people. We need a plan." The set of Jesse's jaw was firm. "We need to go back to the safehouse, Q. You know it."

Quinn hated that Jesse was right. His shoulders slumped, and he nodded, bowing his head as he walked away.

CHAPTER TWELVE

The night before Kat had stumbled around the covered loading dock at the back of Walmart, unable to find a door in the dark. Hearing the approaching crunch of boots she'd darted behind a forklift as the beam of two flashlights came around the corner.

"Charlie's taking bets on how many we're going to find," a strange voice said.

"Charlie's a sadistic bastard. Don't you feel bad about trapping people here and then taking them?" a second unfamiliar voice responded.

"Nah. It's easier than going door-to-door in the towns."

"I just think we should give them a choice about coming with us."

There was a loud chortle. "Don't let the boss catch you talking like that."

They walked straight to a door that Kat saw had a hand-painted sign: SUPPLIES INSIDE. TAKE WHAT YOU NEED.

They were trapping people? Shivering with fear and

cold, Kat watched as they pulled handguns and entered the building.

They were gone for ten minutes, and it was just the two of them who returned.

"First time we haven't found any."

"Maybe we've picked up everyone who's still alive."

"You wish. We'll be back out again tomorrow, looking for more."

"Did you re-set the latch?"

"Of course I fucking did."

They walked away, taking the light with them.

Kat crouched down, shaking. So much for spending the night in there. She was weak with hunger and exhaustion, and didn't know if she had the strength to walk far for shelter. And something was seriously wrong with her hip. She figured she wouldn't be walking on it if it was broken, but there had to be some kind of internal bruising or ligament damage.

She waited, her body seizing up in the cold, but the soldiers didn't leave. When it finally dawned on her they were staying the night, she cried. She could barely move. If she'd stayed in the truck, she'd at least have the body warmth of the other captives.

Why could she never make the right decision?

Her sight had finally adjusted to the dark, and she inched her way to the side of the building and around, monitoring the truck and jeep as she scouted for a vehicle she could hide inside. The first car she tried was locked, and she cried harder at the energy she'd exerted to scrape away the built-up snow.

Her hands were raw and probably frost-bitten.

Swallowing back her sobs she tried the next vehicle,

which looked like an old pickup truck. Her fingernails were broken and bleeding by the time she reached the door handle and she whimpered with relief when it opened. Crawling into the cab, she collapsed as the door snicked closed behind her. She'd landed on a pile of something soft– a down-filled puffer jacket.

In her eagerness to pull on the over-sized jacket she knocked her knee into the glove-box, wincing at the sharp pain. The glove-box... Holding her breath she clicked it open, exhaling in a loud rush when she felt around and pulled out a pair of fleece-lined gloves.

Puffing with exertion she sat back against the seat, spent.

She had nothing left.

It was warmer inside the cab, the snow that encased it turning it into a kind of insulated igloo. The additional layer of the second jacket was enough to stop her shivering and, before she knew it, exhaustion took over and she fell asleep.

DAY 69

THE TRUCK ROARING to life the next morning woke Kat. From the small patch of ice and snow she'd scraped away from the window last night, she could see the truck and jeep pull away.

Her heart lifted.

She'd escaped, stayed undetected, and hadn't frozen to death last night.

Now, she just had to make it back to the safehouse and admit her mistakes.

Somewhere over the last forty-eight hours she had

owned up to the negative impact her behavior had on those who loved her. It wasn't just sneaking out to single-handedly solve Chloe's problems, and the unforgivable damage that had caused. She'd been dismissing the actions of her consequences for as long as she could remember.

It was time to step up. She didn't deserve forgiveness, but she hoped for understanding. Until she got that, she would work to make things right. And that started with bringing back the bodies of Sami, Jimmy and Lucas, and giving them the dignity of a proper farewell.

Determined, she pushed to open the door of the pickup, braced for the cold air and the challenge ahead of her.

The door didn't open.

It didn't budge under her repeated shoves.

Something caught her eye, two men walking around the area the soldiers had camped. She instantly froze. Had they come back?

The size of one of the men, his height and the breadth of his shoulders, made her blink. And blink again. Was she imagining things? And then he turned as he threw his arms in the air and she bashed her shoulder against the stuck door. "Quinn! Quinn!"

The door held fast.

Gasping, she watched in horror as Quinn and Jesse appeared to argue, and then Quinn's shoulders slumped and his head bowed.

And he walked away.

"No. No! Quinn! I'm here!" She smashed her fists against the glass of the window and then fell onto her back so she could kick out at the door. She was a crazed person, kicking and screaming and punching.

Sweating and shattered, she finally gave up, collapsing

against the armrest with her face pressed against the small patch of clear glass.

There was no one there. They were long gone.

She cried then. Big gulping sobs of grief and fear and frustration.

She'd made a mess of everything, and now even Quinn had given up on her.

She hadn't allowed herself to hope he would come, but somewhere deep inside she must have. The memory of his bowed head ruined her.

Finally, she sat back in the seat and stared at the stained ceiling of the pickup.

Why wouldn't the door open? She worried at the problem like a child with a loose tooth. The sunshine yesterday had made the snow slushier; had the freezing temperature last night then re-frozen the slushy snow around the hinges of the door?

If so, did that mean she just had to wait it out until the sun warmed the snow again?

Could she run out of oxygen in here?

That just made her breathing speed up and the panic return.

She took a deep breath. And then another one, sitting up straight.

Okay, she could deal with this. Wasn't this what she had just been promising herself? That she would change– slow down and base her decisions on thought, rather than emotion.

It hurt, deep in her soul, that Quinn had given up.

She loved how he'd adored her–for the first time in her life she believed she could be worthy; he'd accepted her even with her faults and flaws. And it was okay that his feelings weren't as forever as he'd let her believe they were.

She didn't blame him; she hadn't been the person who could inspire that kind of devotion.

But she would be.

Because Quinn was worth it. *She* was worth it.

And honestly, if cauliflower could somehow become pizza, then Kat could do anything. She could change. She just had to get out of this pickup.

———

"YOU'VE GOT TO BE KIDDING!" Quinn slammed his hands down on the steering wheel. The gas gauge had been in the red for longer than comfortable, but he'd been sure they could get it back to the safehouse.

The heating cut out as the four-wheel drive coasted to a stop.

"Where are you from again?" he asked Jesse.

Jesse raised an eyebrow. "Down south. Why?"

"Is it warmer there?"

"Sure as hell doesn't snow like this."

Quinn shook his head, gazing out at the winter-dominated streets. "We can't do another season like this. We need to leave the mid-west."

"Good luck getting the others to agree to that. Didn't you grow up with this kind of weather?"

"I grew up with electricity and roads that were plowed daily."

Jesse huffed a laugh, conceding Quinn's point. "So, what now?"

"Now, we walk back to that Land Rover dealership. I've always wanted to drive one of their Defenders." He looked at Jesse. "Ever owned a hundred and thirty thousand dollar vehicle?"

"What do you think?" Jesse got out of the four-wheel drive, shaking his head.

The snow was slushy and made the going harder, further resolving Quinn to move to a state with no snow. This was bullshit.

The dealership relied on electricity for their security and without it, the automatic glass entrance doors pushed open easily. A foot of built-up snow fell onto the polished concrete floor and Quinn stepped over it, breathing in the scent of money and new car.

Even weeks after the collapse of society, the dealership retained its gleaming surfaces and general air of luxury.

Jesse whistled.

"This one." Quinn ran his hand reverently over the hood of a fully loaded silver V8 Carpathian Edition Defender.

"You know the keys to that are probably in a computerized locked storage cabinet, right?" Jesse asked, heading to the glassed-in sales offices at the back.

"And you know we're in an apocalypse, and can just smash it open, right?" Quinn followed him, anxious to get going. The acquisition of a luxury car didn't detract from the feverish urgency to rescue Kat.

As he'd predicted, brute force had him holding up the correct key fob in minutes.

"Let's go."

"So, we just drive it out the front?" Jesse eyed the door in question. "Will it fit?"

"How do you think it got in here?"

Quinn didn't have the time or concentration to appreciate the pure elegance of the vehicle, he simply adjusted the seat to accommodate his length and pressed the ignition.

It purred to life as Jesse climbed into the passenger side.

"What horsepower does this baby have?" Jesse began fiddling with the dashboard controls.

"It's five-liter supercharged," Quinn said, distracted as he manoeuvred around the showroom floor and into the empty exterior lot.

"Do you think we should go by the liquor store, and get the bodies?" Jesse asked, leaving the buttons and screens and sitting back in the seat. "I hate the idea of them being there."

"So do I, and we will. But not now. We don't know if the Panthers are still in that area, or if the others have already been and collected them. And Kat is my priority."

They'd only been driving minutes when Quinn stamped on the brake, the Defender veering wildly.

"What is it?"

"Something's going on up ahead." Quinn pulled his Ruger. "Those are our snowmobiles, sitting in the middle of the street."

"The Panthers have abandoned them?" Jesse lowered his window so he could rest his rifle through it, lowering his head to look through the scope. "Nah, that blonde chick is standing to the left, you see her? Missy, that's her name."

"Anyone else?"

"Not that I can see. But she wouldn't be by herself." Jesse looked up. "What do we do? Backtrack?"

"Too risky, they could see us." Quinn wanted to bellow in frustration. Everything was one step forward, two steps back. And every hold-up ratcheted the tension inside him until he didn't know how much more he could handle.

"So what? We just sit here?"

"They're half a block away and facing the opposite direction. So yeah, we just sit here. Unless you'd rather keep walking in the snow?" Quinn snarled.

Jesse went quiet and Quinn sighed. "Sorry, it's shitty to take my anger out on you."

"It's okay, man. I get it."

"Check that out," Quinn breathed, eyes widening at a truck barrelling towards Missy with an enormous snowplow emblazoned with the word MALLRATS. It picked up speed, pushing anything and everything from its path with horrific ease.

The noise was intense, even from a distance.

Missy stood her ground, and several Panthers emerged from surrounding buildings to flank her.

"Did we just get ourselves stuck in the middle of their war?" Jesse flashed Quinn a worried look. "Because I'm not cool with this."

"We can't afford to move now. Even getting out and running could draw their attention. If they look like they're coming this way, we run across to that laundromat–see it? We went through it yesterday and there's a door to a back alley, remember? We'll have enough of a head-start to get away."

Jesse nodded without looking at the laundromat, riveted to the unfolding scene ahead of them. A nondescript man of average height got down from the Mallrat truck, smiling blandly.

"I did *not* expect that," Jesse murmured.

Missy stepped up to the man, and the two started talking. Missy's sharp hand gestures radiated animosity, but the Mallrat was unaffected. If anything, he looked bored.

"You think it's some kind of deal? Are they negotiating?" Quinn shifted in his seat, wishing he could hear what was being said.

"They're taking their sweet time." Jesse leaned back further and propped a boot up on the dash.

"Get your foot down." Quinn sent him a scathing look. "That's no way to treat a vehicle like this."

Ignoring him, Jesse shut his eyes. "I know this is a tense situation, but we're just bystanders. And man, I am *so* tired."

Exhaustion tugged at Quinn, too, but he pushed it back. "Thanks for coming with me. You didn't have to, and I appreciate it."

"I know I didn't grow up with y'all, but after all this? I feel like we're family, you know?"

Quinn nodded slowly. He did know.

"And if Kat hadn't done what she did..."

"Chloe would have left." Quinn finished.

"Yeah." Jesse sighed heavily.

"And you're really okay with raising another man's baby?"

"What do you think?" Jesse snapped his eyes open. "Of course I am." Settling back he closed his eyes again. "You watching out there? What's happening?"

"More of the same. If they could just take each other out, that would be helpful."

"Who knew the end of the world would turn everyone into assholes?"

Quinn barked out a laugh, surprising himself. "At least they aren't zombies. That would really suck."

"Yeah, you're right." Jesse nodded seriously. "Especially if they were the fast moving ones like in *The Last of Us*. I reckon I could take the slow zombies in *The Walking Dead*, but those fast ones are scary."

"Hold up, they're moving." Quinn adjusted his rifle scope as Jesse jerked upright. "They're leaving." He couldn't believe his eyes. Not a single shot had been fired, and both gangs were backing away from each other and going their separate ways.

Stunned, he and Jesse sat in silence, until the street ahead was clear.

And then they started for home.

CHAPTER THIRTEEN

Kat really was a new woman. The second house she broke into had several unopened bottles of wine on the kitchen table, and she didn't glance at them twice.

She had to stop using alcohol to mask her problems, and that started now.

Unfortunately, this garage was also empty.

The frustration rising in her called for the wine. *Begged* for the wine.

Resolutely she trudged to the next house.

The door was locked, but the key was under the doormat. Kat said a quick thanks to stupid people and let herself inside.

The same stupid people were sitting on the sofa, dead.

Kat screamed, dropping the bottle of water she'd picked up at the first house.

It was a man and a woman, badly decomposed but with obvious bullet holes in their heads. Winter had frozen them in this macabre state, masking the smell of death.

Kat gulped and ran through the open-plan living space to the kitchen, where she leant against the island counter, gasping. When she finally calmed, she spotted a box of Cheerios and picked it up, hugging it to her chest.

Munching on the dry cereal she inspected the door to the left. Pantry. Door to the right. Laundry. Door in the laundry? Garage. Bingo.

Inside the dark space sat a blue RAV4. It didn't have snow tires and there weren't any in the garage that she could find, but she doubted she had the strength or ability to swap them anyway.

She was desperate.

Surely it wouldn't be too hard to drive in the snow in normal tires? It wasn't ideal, but it was possible, right?

Keys hung from a hook at the door and Kat grabbed them, crossing her fingers the SUV would start. When it did, she almost didn't believe her luck. She sighed when the luck didn't extend to finding a street map in the vehicle, but she hadn't really expected it to. With GPS on smartphones, no one needed paper maps anymore.

Well, they hadn't.

It didn't matter. She could navigate her way back to the safehouse.

Kat pushed the garage door remote, already putting on her seat belt. When the door didn't open she looked into the rearview mirror in confusion, hitting the button again.

She groaned. Goddamn lack of electricity! How did people in the olden days survive?

"It's okay, it's okay, it's okay," she chanted, getting out to inspect the inside of the door. There was an emergency release cord, and she pulled on it experimentally. There was a clanking sound, as though the door was disconnecting from something. When she tugged on the bottom of the door, it slid upwards and sunlight poured into the garage.

Kat pirouetted, punching the air.

She danced back to the idling car and climbed inside, slipping on a pair of sunglasses she found in the console.

She could do this.

The realization she was close, so close, was a sudden ache in her heart. She rubbed the heel of her hand against chest. These people–her found-family–were everything to her. But would they take her back? She'd not only caused the deaths of Sami, Jimmy and Lucas, but she'd run like a coward. Leaving Cassie and Stephen. Leaving everyone.

She looked down at the steering wheel. She could take this car and leave town, start somewhere else… out there. And she wouldn't have to face her failures and the condemnation of the people she loved most in the world.

Maybe that was the best option. And sure as shit it was what the old Kat would've done.

"HOLY SHIIIIIIIT!"

The rear wheels of the RAV4 lost traction and the entire vehicle began sliding sideways into an embankment of snow, with Kat frantically pumping the brake and pulling on the steering wheel.

It lodged against the embankment with a thunk and she threw her hands in the air and her head back against the headrest.

She'd remembered when Jake was driving the school bus, he'd said that when driving in snow it was better to use second gear rather first. Something about first gear having too much torque–whatever that meant.

She'd been so careful.

And yet this was the third time she'd lost control in the slushy snow. It was *impossible*.

Gritting her teeth, she started her chanting again. It was going to be okay.

But this time when she tried to drive out of the situation, the tires just spun uselessly. She didn't move an inch.

"Fuck!" It was hard to stay positive and motivated when everything was so damn *hard*.

Fine. She got out of the RAV and slammed the door. She'd walk.

It sucked. Every step was an effort, and she was wet to above her knees. She was sweating and her hip was on fire and she was so. damn. tired.

She stopped, bending over at the waist and gasping in the icy air. When she straightened, a street sign with graffiti at the end of the road caught her eye.

No way. That was *her* graffiti. Always Forever marked the sign like a beacon of hope and suddenly the pain in her hip, the cold, all disappeared. Holy shit. She was really going to do this.

It wasn't until she was standing in front of the safe-house, trembling and close to collapse, that Kat let herself stop. She'd been concentrating so hard on getting here, that she hadn't allowed herself to think about what kind of reception she would receive.

Her heart lodged in her throat.

Old Kat was fearless, but new Kat was fearless, *and* she knew the consequences of being brave. She was also strong enough to face this.

Gripping the stair rail, she dragged herself up the stairs and with a shaking hand opened the front door. Inside was chaos, with Dex barking, people running and orders shouted.

"... get that extra gas container."

"Did you put water on that list?"

"Oh, hey." Mackenzie stuck her head into the hall, spotting Kat. "Rach needs help with matching the ammo with the guns we–" Her eyes widened. "Fuck. Fuck-fuck-fuckity-fuck. Kat!" She dropped the box she was holding and began screaming and crying, running to Kat and bowling her over.

Kat's hip shrieked in agony but she clutched Mackenzie tighter, the two of them a tangle of limbs on the floor.

"You're here. Oh my god, you're here!" Mackenzie wailed. "We thought we'd lost you."

Kat had no words. Tears leaked from her eyes but she just held Mackenzie closer.

"How did you get here?" Mackenzie finally pulled away, helping them both to their feet. "You look like shit, babe."

"Thanks." Kat rolled her eyes. "What's going on?" She looked up as footsteps ran back and forth in the room above them.

"We're coming to rescue you," Mackenzie said simply.

"Mac, did you get... oh. Oh!" Chloe flew down the stairs and launched herself at Kat, the two only staying upright because Mackenzie caught them both.

"Rach! Get out here!" Mackenzie called.

"I'm kind of busy," Rachel shouted back.

Kat laughed into Chloe's shoulder, legs wobbly and a deep, deep gratitude flowing through her veins for these women she called family.

"Rachel Davenport, get your ass out here!" Mackenzie was grinning widely.

"Mac, we don't have time–" Rachel stopped in the hallway, blinking. And then her whole face crumpled and she stood there, gulping air and crying–great heaving sobs that wracked her body.

James ran up behind her and turned her into his chest,

wrapped his arms around her. When he looked up and saw Kat his mouth dropped open.

Kat smiled at him weakly.

When Chloe let her go she wobbled.

"God, you need to sit down." Chloe fussed and led her towards the kitchen, but Kat stopped her.

"Cassie and Stephen," she whispered. "Are they... okay?"

"They're going to be fine," Mackenzie said gently, taking Kat's other arm.

With James leading a sniffling Rachel, Mackenzie and Chloe supported Kat and followed them into the kitchen. Before Kat could fall into a chair Rachel had engulfed her.

"I love you," she whispered fiercely into Kat's hair. "And no matter what happens, I will *always* love you."

The screech of a chair being pushed back caught Kat's attention, and she glanced over to see Stephen slowly standing, Cassie at his side.

Rachel gave her space so Kat could turn to face them.

Words stuck in her throat.

"It wasn't your fault, Kat," Stephen said, putting his arm around Cassie.

"I'm sorry. I'm so, so sorry," Kat whispered.

"We chose to go with you," Cassie said, her own eyes filling with tears. "And you didn't pull the trigger. You didn't kill them."

Their grace was Kat's undoing, and she collapsed at their feet, lightheaded and trembling.

James was quick to pick her up and help her onto a chair, where Chloe knelt before her, taking her hands.

"What you did..."

"I'm sorry, Chlo. I was irresponsible and–"

"You were selfless and loyal," Chloe squeezed her

fingers. "But you broke my heart. Kat, I'm allowed to risk my life, you're not allowed to risk yours for me."

"I will risk anything for you," Kat said. She looked around at the others. "I will risk anything for all of you."

As full as her heart was, she was still missing something. Where was Quinn?

———

"IN DIFFERENT CIRCUMSTANCES, this could be the best day of my life." Jake stepped into the Land Rover dealership, Quinn and Jesse on his heels.

He grunted when Quinn shoved an elbow into his side.

"Sorry. Not appropriate, I know. But seriously, I didn't even drive one of these in my dreams."

Scowling, Quinn strode to the smashed cabinet and picked out key fobs for the other two Defenders. He wanted to be in and out as quick as possible.

Heading back to the row of shiny new vehicles he tossed a key each to Jake and Jesse.

"The sooner we're back, the sooner we can go after Kat," he growled. "So get your head in the game."

He didn't wait for them to start the Defenders, just jogged back to where he'd parked his. The urgent need to get moving, to do something, thrummed through his blood.

He drove faster than was smart back to the safehouse, impatient to get everyone loaded and moving. He swore when he pulled in at the curb; he'd been expecting people moving about and gear stacked and ready to be loaded, but there was nothing.

What the hell were they doing?

When he stormed inside, it was still and quiet.

"Where the fuck is everyone?" he yelled.

"Keep it down! She's sleeping." Chloe emerged from the living room, her brow creased. "Oh, hey." Her forehead smoothed. "Come with me."

Panic brewed in Quinn's gut when Chloe took his hand and tugged him forward. What was going on?

The drapes had been drawn in the living space and walking in it took a moment for Quinn's eyes to adjust. When they did, he looked down and saw a bundled form on the sofa, snoring softly.

The shock of seeing Kat's sweet face, relaxed in sleep, destroyed him. His legs gave out, and he fell to his knees, the floor shuddering with the impact at the same time his heart expanded in his chest. He fought to draw a deep breath.

How was this possible?

Was he dreaming?

Confused and afraid, he looked to Chloe. "It's her."

"Uh huh." Chloe nodded gently. "I'll give you guys your privacy."

The door clicked shut behind Chloe and Quinn stared helplessly at Kat, afraid to touch her in case he woke up and once again found himself in the nightmare reality of being without her.

She was so fragile and pale, with dark purple circles beneath her eyes, and her hands resting atop the blankets were bandaged.

Carefully, he swept her knotted hair back from her face.

"I swear you will never face anything alone again," he whispered.

Her lashes fluttered open, and she stared at him. "You came."

"I will *always* come for you."

She closed her eyes and smiled. "Take me to bed?"

Standing, he gathered her, blankets and all, holding her reverently against his chest. He was holding his whole world in his hands.

"Careful," she groaned. "My hip is really banged up."

"And your hands?"

She raised one to rest on his bearded cheek.

"Rach thinks I've got mild frostbite. They're discolored and blistered, but there shouldn't be permanent damage."

Quinn's shoulders shook. He had no words.

Sensing his distress, Kat gazed into his eyes. "They didn't hurt me. Not more than my hip, anyway. The frostbite is my own fault."

"Darlin', you need to take better care of yourself." His voice was hoarse with unshed tears. "Because I can't live without you."

DAY 73

KAT WAS adorable when she was cantankerous.

Quinn grinned as she crossed her arms over her chest. She scowled when she had to drop them, because the bandages on her hands were too bulky.

"This is ridiculous! It's been days. I am not an invalid, I can get out of bed," she whined.

"Rachel said–"

"Do not say 'Rachel said' to me! I'm telling you that I'm fine." She smacked the top of the blankets to emphasize her point, and then winced.

"Still hurt, huh?" Quinn climbed onto the bed with her, taking her hands and kissing the bandages.

She pulled them away, cross. "I swear to god, Quinn!

You won't let me out of bed, you won't have sex with me, you won't–"

He cut her off with his mouth, slanting his lips over hers and kissing away her petulance. She melted beneath him as he deepened the kiss, sliding his tongue inside as she opened for him.

They kissed, wet and deep, losing themselves in the promise of their own forever.

Breathless, she pushed at his chest. "If you don't have sex with me *right now*, I'm going to take matters into my own hands." To prove her point, she began biting at the ends of her bandage.

"Stop, you little minx." He grabbed her wrists and held her still. "I have a surprise for you."

"Does it involve your D and my V?" She batted her eyelashes.

"It involves getting out of bed," he conceded.

"Oh, well. That's a close second. I'll take it." She slid her legs from beneath the covers and stood, only wobbling slightly.

When he started forward, she waved him off. "I'm fine."

"Dress warm, we're going outside."

She raised her eyebrows, surprised. And then grinned. "You going to help me with that?"

"No, you brat. We'll never get out of bed if I get you naked," he chuckled. "Rach is going to come and take your bandages off, and then you can get changed. I'll meet you downstairs."

He brushed a kiss over her forehead, anticipation buzzing through him.

Rachel met him at the door to the bedroom, laden down with medical supplies. At his worried look, she rolled her eyes. "Her hands are going to be good as new."

She pushed past him and shut the door in his face.

Quinn paced downstairs, running through his mental checklist.

"Dude, what's got you so jacked up?" Jake looked up from the sofa he was sprawled on, Mackenzie's head in his lap.

"I'm taking Kat somewhere. Can you distract Rachel?"

"Are you doing something stupid?" Jake sighed.

"No, it's safe. You know I wouldn't jeopardize her. Jesse and I staked it out yesterday and I checked again just now. It's fine."

"Where are you going?" Mackenzie popped her head up.

"None of your business." Quinn picked up his gloves and wound Kat's scarf around his neck.

"It is if you want our help with Rach." She grinned cheekily at him.

"Help me with what?" Rachel came down the stairs, followed by Kat who waggled her unbandaged fingers at him.

Quinn sighed. "I'm taking Kat out."

"What? Where? No." Rachel frowned. "We only go out for essentials, you know that."

"This is essential." Quinn took Kat's hand and passed her the gloves he'd looted yesterday. They were fur-lined leather with a cashmere interior. He'd nearly dropped them when he'd seen their price tag.

"Ooo, these are pretty," Kat cooed, pulling them on.

"Quinn–" Rachel started.

He flipped her the bird and walked out of the house, a giggling Kat holding his arm.

"She's going to make you regret that," Kat warned.

"I regret nothing when it comes to you."

He opened the passenger door to the Defender and helped her inside, waving to Jesse sitting in another Defender. He was going to follow them and wait a half block down, keeping a lookout.

Quinn was serious about not taking any chances.

Getting into the driver's seat he double-checked his rifle and got the vehicle running, adjusting the vents so warm air was blowing over Kat.

"You feeling okay?" he asked.

"I'm amazing. This is a *really* nice car." She was stroking the leather seat and gazing around the spacious interior. "You wanna fuck on the back seat?"

"Yes." He grinned. "But not right now."

"So what's worth risking Rachel's wrath for? Where are we going?"

"Not far."

When he pulled up beside an upscale boutique, Kat clapped her hands. "More gloves?" Her hand went to the door handle, and he gave her a stern look. "Darlin', if you don't wait for me to open your door, I'm going to be pissed."

Striding around to her door he opened it, swinging her out and into his arms. Down the block, Jesse stopped and flashed his lights. Good to go.

Beside the boutique was a small bespoke jewelery store, its fancy gold logo discreetly stamped on the door. Quinn had broken in yesterday to find the keys to all the glass display cases, so the door swung open easily when he carried Kat inside.

She gasped at the candles he'd placed around the well-appointed interior, the glass cabinets reflecting a warm glow that amplified the sparkling gems within.

Quinn set her on her feet and then lowered himself until he was kneeling before her.

"Quinn?"

He wiped sweating hands on his jeans and swallowed.

"Kat. You are my end, and my beginning. You are my everything." His voice caught, and he swallowed again. "Will you be my wife?"

Her mouth parted in a perfect 'o' of surprise. "You love me that much?"

"More than you could ever imagine."

"You know I'm not perfect." Her lower lip trembled.

"I love you just the way you are."

"You want to marry me?"

"I want to marry you. But, darlin'? My leg is cramping. Can you say yes so I can get up?" His mouth twitched, and then he couldn't hold back his smile. "Please?"

"Yes. Yes!" She laughed. "Yes, I will marry you."

In a flash he was on his feet, and she squealed as he swept her into his arms. He spun her in circles until her arms were wrapped tight around his neck and he was kissing her senseless.

When they finally broke apart, panting, she wiggled to be put down. He lowered her slowly, letting her body slide tantalizingly against his own.

"I need you to pick out a ring. And then I need inside your pussy."

"The ring can wait." She unzipped her jacket.

He stepped back, shaking his head. "The ring *can not* wait. When I fuck my fiancé, she's going to be wearing a diamond on her finger."

"Okay, that one." She pointed randomly, but then something caught her eye. "Oh. No, *this* one."

Pressing himself to her back he leant over her shoulder, examining the square-cut pink diamond she was staring at.

"Sure you don't want to look around? There are more

displays over there." He nudged her head to the left. "And over there." Nudge to the right.

"Nope. This one."

She was adamant, and he hoped like hell it was the right size. Reaching into the case he plucked the ring from its velvet box, turning to face Kat.

"Hang on." She shook her hair out of its ponytail, pulling at the black hairband. "Give me your hand." When he held it out she stretched the hairband over his wrist, pushing it to sit beside her cheerleading one. "There. Now you're mine as much as I'm yours."

"Darlin' I've always been yours." And he slipped the diamond onto her finger.

CHAPTER FOURTEEN

DAY 75

They had buried Sami, Jimmy and Lucas the day before, under an ancient elm tree in the backyard of the safehouse. The graves weren't as deep as anyone would have liked, but the frozen ground made it next to impossible to dig.

The sun had shone and words were said, remembering the too-short lives of three funny, smart and courageous humans. They mourned the loss of possibility, the loss of friendship and the forfeiture of yet another piece of the old world.

Kat had wanted to postpone the trip to the bridal boutique, knowing that everyone was still raw from yesterday, but the girls didn't agree.

So they were currently being transported in the Defenders to try on wedding gowns, with a marriage ceremony scheduled for next week.

"This is kind of insane," she said, clinking her champagne glass against Chloe's. "Who gets married in an apocalypse?"

"You do. Now shut up, we all need this." Chloe drank deeply of her non-alcoholic bubbles.

Kat looked to Cassie, who was sipping quietly.

"You okay?" she mouthed to the teen.

"Chloe is right," Cassie said. "After everything that's happened... it's good to be celebrating."

"Quinn is marrying you, right or wrong," Jesse called from the driver's seat. "So buckle up, Kat. This is happening."

"Cheers!" James held up a bottle of beer from the passenger seat.

Kat twisted her head to look behind at Quinn driving the other Defender, with Jake, Stephen, Rachel and Mackenzie.

"So you guys are just going to stand around outside while I try on wedding dresses?" Kat leaned forward between the front seats.

"Yep. And drink beer," Jesse responded.

James shot him a look. "We're your *lookouts*. So you can relax and have fun inside, knowing we've got your back."

In the days that Kat had spent in bed recovering, they'd sent out recon teams to discover the locations of both the Panthers and the Mallrats, to guarantee they didn't stray into their territories.

They'd also made a trip to City Hall, looking for documentation and maps of the countryside surrounding Dutton. Stephen and James had spent most of their time since pouring over them, making a shortlist of possible locations they could move to.

No one wanted to stay in Dutton any longer than necessary.

"Okay, this is it." Jesse brought the Defender to a stop in

front of a store with frothing white confections gracing the windows.

"That is a lot of tulle." Kat gulped at the last of her champagne, and then regretted how quickly she'd downed it. She'd promised herself she'd only have one glass.

Quinn pulled in beside them and everyone piled out, Mackenzie and Rachel already giggly from the champagne they'd consumed on the way.

Quinn slung his rifle over his shoulder and walked to Kat, ducking to brush a kiss over her forehead. "I want you to have fun, darlin'. You deserve it."

Kat lit up from the inside, knowing the effort he had gone to. He and Jake had hooked up a generator so not only did they have lights and heat inside, but he'd stocked a mini-fridge with more bottles of champagne and set up a stereo system so they had music.

"You're kind of perfect, you know that?" She brushed a hand over the softness of his beard, blushing as she remembered the feel of it between her legs just that morning.

"Come on, let's do this!" Mackenzie danced into the store, and Kat laughed as Rachel grabbed her hand.

Together they walked into a fairy wonderland of twinkling lights and soft chiffon drapes. Pristine white gowns lined the walls and in the middle, surrounded by elegant velvet armchairs, was a raised dais.

For the next hour, the girls chose dresses and made Kat try them on, everything from ridiculously poufy creations, to slinky satin and classic princess-style dresses. Kat twirled on the dais to exclamations and raised champagne glasses, all the while knowing which dress she wanted.

It hung on a mannequin off to the side–a soft dusky pink with an exquisitely detailed French lace strapless bodice, falling into an airy tulle ballgown silhouette with delicate beading, that swept the floor decadently.

"How are you ever going to pick one?" Cassie was flushed and gorgeously tipsy, lying on a fluffy white floor rug.

"Unzip me?" Kat turned her back to Mackenzie, who complied. Letting the dress fall from her body she walked in her underwear to the pink gown, holding it to her front and turning to face the girls. "This one."

"Oh!" Chloe held a hand to her chest, her eyes brimming. "I'm sorry, I can't stop crying! I love it."

"It's perfect," said Rachel, coming to help Kat step into the gown. "It's exactly what I imagined you wearing." She spun Kat by the shoulder so she could see herself in the floor-length mirror and Kat inhaled.

It really was perfect.

"Everyone out!" Quinn thundered from the front door, causing shrieks of alarm.

"What! What is it?" Mackenzie yelled, dropping her glass.

"I need five minutes with my bride," Quinn demanded, eyes on Kat as he stalked forward.

"Quinn, you can't–" Chloe broke off when Quinn shot her a dark look.

Kat watched him advance on her through the mirror, the girls laughing as they hurriedly exited, leaving them alone with the soft beat of jazz coming through the speakers.

He came to stand behind her, eyes ravenous as they devoured her.

She licked her lips.

"I couldn't wait." His voice was hoarse, his desire barely

restrained. He stroked a thumb over his bottom lip, suggestive. Provocative.

Kat's pussy clenched, and heat flooded her, knowing exactly what havoc those lips could cause.

His hands, so big, stroked down her shoulders and across her collarbones, leaving gooseflesh in their wake.

"You like?" she whispered, unable to look away from his caressing touch.

"I like." His words dripped with sexual intent. "I know we said we'd wait until we were married, but I want you pregnant and carrying my baby."

"Okay."

"Okay?" His hands stilled. "I can fuck you bare?"

She turned into him, rising on her toes so she could draw his face down to hers. "Only if you do it right. fucking. now."

He growled, pushing her against the mirror and biting into her cleavage as his hands dove beneath the voluminous skirt of her dress, bunching it high as he found the silk of her panties and ripped them off.

She moaned, rocking into his hand as his fingers found her pussy, plunging into her wetness and setting off fireworks behind her closed eyelids. Her bodice slipped to expose her tits and Quinn sucked and tongued her tight nipples, causing her to throw her head back in abandonment. She felt debaucherously wild, disheveled and half-naked, and so very, very alive.

He lifted her legs to wrap around his hips, pushing at the layers of tulle until the crown of his cock was breaching her, stretching her wide.

Their eyes caught, held.

"Fuck me," she begged.

His hands holding her ass guided her down, down, until

she was fully seated and gloriously full. His hands framed her face, and he worshiped her lips with his.

"I've never been bare with someone before," he muttered into her neck. "It's the most intense feeling. I'm not going to last long, darlin'."

She gyrated her pelvis, slow and sure. "Better get started then, big boy."

Laughing, he bit her throat. "You did not just call me that."

She responded with another gyration.

He growled, all teeth and barely leashed power. Pulling back he thrust forward, his cock slamming into her. Again and again. She clung to him, in awe of his strength and his restraint as he fucked into her until the building wave of her orgasm crested, and crashed over her, robbing her of coherent thought.

Quinn climaxed with a shout, the last drive of his cock pulsating with his release.

Forehead to forehead, they breathed each other in.

"I love you," she whispered.

He stilled. "That's the first time you've told me that."

"No, it's not," she scoffed, pulling back to see him properly. "I've said it before."

"Nope. That was the first time." He kissed the corner of her mouth. "Can you say it again?"

"I can't believe I haven't told you already. Of course I love you." She pulled his face closer by his beard and ground their mouths together. "I love you," she mumbled against him.

He smacked her on the ass and then released her, lifting her from his cock and setting her gently on her feet. She rearranged the wedding gown, luxuriating in the feel of his cum between her legs and accepting the panties he passed her.

Satisfied she looked presentable, she smacked him lightly on the chest. "You know you're not meant to see my dress before the day."

"I can't wait for you to be my wife."

And she couldn't wait for him to be her husband. She knew without an official celebrant the law wouldn't recognize their marriage. But what was the law now, anyway? They would be married in the eyes of their family, and that was all that mattered.

"Let's just do it. Here. Now. I don't want to wait," she burst out.

"What?"

"Everyone we love is already here. I'm dressed, there's music and fairy lights. Let's do it."

"Darlin', are you sure?"

Happiness welled within her. "I want to start my forever with you."

THE END

Read on for the prologue of *After The End*, the final book in The After post-apocalyptic series.
PRE-ORDER NOW!

PROLOGUE | AFTER THE END
BOOK #4

DAY 1

Ash sighed heavily, putting his cell phone back in the inside pocket of his suit jacket.

"The wife again?" Hilary's question wasn't innocent, and Ash regretted ever confiding in her about his marital... issues.

"Not now, Hil. What the hell is going on in here?"

The foyer of the JW Marriott Hotel was chaotic; there was a frantic edge to people's movements and open desperation on their faces.

Ash's concern morphed to alarm when a bellhop shoved his luggage trolley at a red-faced woman and walked out the front doors into the teaming foot traffic of a New York City morning.

The pounding in his head intensified and a coughing fit took him.

"Here." Hilary passed him a bottle of water. "Looks like you've got whatever's going around."

Ash wiped his watering eyes.

"I'm fine. Where's Brian? Did you get concierge to book a cab?"

"I don't know where he is, but while you were... *placating* your wife, the client called. The meeting has been canceled. Everyone is either sick or getting sick." Hilary opened her purse and passed him a blister pack of Tylenol.

"Seriously?" That meant extra days in New York and an extra pissed off wife.

Chloe was already suggesting he look for a career without the extensive travel associated with being a management consultant. Problem was, Ash loved his job. He was good at providing strategic advice to companies on improving operational efficiency. Really good. And the pay was exceptional.

Chloe wasn't complaining about that part of his job.

"So Brian's sick?" Ash checked his watch. If their meeting was cancelled, maybe he could move up the meeting with HR. Head office was in New York, and they'd been courting him to move here. He knew Chloe would flip her lid at the suggestion of leaving their hometown of Sanford, but he'd be stupid to not at least see what kind of offer they had on the table.

"That's him now." Hilary turned to watch Brian puff his way over to them, his paunch belly emphasized by an ill-positioned belt. "He really should hit the gym with us more," she muttered under her breath.

"Have you seen the news?" Brian gasped, taking the water bottle from Ash's hands and gulping at it.

"Hey, man. You really shouldn't have done that. I'm not feeling so great." Ash grimaced as Brian dropped the bottle and water spilled over the marble floor.

"You're sick?" Brian's face blanched white.

"It's just that flu everyone's getting." Ash bit back a cough.

"It's not a flu! They're calling it Sy-V, and it's *killing* people." Brian took a giant step away from Ash. "We should all go back to our rooms. The less contact we have with other people, the better."

"You can, but if the meeting is canceled then I'm rescheduling my flight," Hilary said. "No point in hanging around here."

Ash didn't like the way she looked at him when she said that. As though she were silently asking if there *was* a reason she should hang around.

Hilary had always been a companionable colleague, but ever since her divorce last year, there had been an undercurrent of *something* that made Ash awkward.

"You don't get it!" Spittle flew from Brian's fleshy mouth. "All flights have been grounded, and LaGuardia and JFK have both been quarantined."

"What? Over the *flu?*" Ash realized this was what Chloe had been so worked up about. If he hadn't done that extra set of reps in his workout this morning, he'd have had time to catch the news.

"I told you! It's not the flu. It's called the Syrian Virus and people are *dying*. It's all over the world." Brian shook his head. "I don't know about you two, but I'm heading back to my room to drink the mini-bar dry."

Ash was already walking to the bank of elevators. He wanted to turn on a television and find out what was really happening.

And he should call Chloe back, too.

"Get your own elevator." Brian pushed in front of him. "I'm not sharing an enclosed space with you."

The elevator dinged and Brian hustled inside, jabbing at the buttons with his elbows.

Ash sighed. Whatever. Brian had always been a jerk.

"We can ride this out together?"

Hilary had come up beside him, a suggestive glint to her eye. Thankfully, a coughing fit had him doubled-up over and her expression quickly changed.

"I'm going to grab a coffee and check my emails. If you're feeling better, I'm in room 807. Call me." She gave a half wave and strode away in heels he couldn't imagine were comfortable.

The elevator doors opened again, disgorging at least ten people, all with luggage and all in a hurry. Many were coughing and one had a bleeding nose.

Ash got in, along with a well-dressed couple speaking in Italian. There was a smear of what looked like blood on one of the mirrored walls, and Ash grimaced, standing well clear of it. When he began coughing again, the couple exchanged disgusted glances and tried to stand well clear of *him*.

A flash of fear lodged in his gut. Did he have this virus? And what did that mean?

The throb of his headache reasserted itself, making it hard to think.

He'd call Chloe, have some more Tylenol, and then lie down.

It took several attempts to use his key card, his hands were shaky, and his vision was getting blurry. When he got into the room he immediately set the thermostat of the air-con to low—he was burning up.

Ditching his jacket, he loosened his tie and rolled up his shirt sleeves, turning on the faucet to splash cold water on his face.

He'd had a cough for a couple of days, but the onset of these symptoms blindsided him with their swiftness. He'd been feeling fine less than twenty minutes ago.

What made him feel even worse was the way he'd fobbed Chloe off. What he wouldn't give to be on a flight home to her right now.

Sitting on the edge of the bed he picked up his cell to call her, but every time he dialed it came up as a network error. Hi jaw ticked and when he opened the internet browser on his cell and saw it was unavailable, he cursed, long and loud.

When he picked up the room telephone to dial out, he only got a busy tone. Frustrated, he slammed the handset down, slumping his shoulders as another coughing fit racked his body.

When he could finally draw a deep breath again, he flicked on the television. While many of the channels just showed static, the Chinese news was still operating, as were the movie channels, and a sport channel showing a British football game.

He stopped his channel hopping when a harried-looking female news presenter filled the screen. Her eyes were red-rimmed and she was speaking so fast it was hard to understand her.

"... unprecedented mortality rates. We've lost contact with Europe, and most countries in the Asia Pacific are under martial law. Until the World Health Organization has information on a vaccine, the President has issued a ruling for a mandatory curfew. No one is to be outside their homes after midday today. I repeat, stay-at-home orders come into effect at midday today, with severe penalties for those breaching the order."

The remote fell from Ash's hand as he stared at the screen in shock.

What the *hell* was going on?

———

PRE-ORDER *After The End* to read Chloe and Ash's story, in the conclusion to The After post-apocalyptic series.

NOVELLA IN THE RUINED WORLD POST-APOCALYPTIC SERIES

RUINED WORLD

JACQUELINE HAYLEY

RUINED WORLD

CHAPTER ONE

DAY 1

"Shit is about to hit the fan. Over."

Noah Ramsey paused before clicking on the ham radio receiver. "Copy. Over."

He pictured his ex-Marine buddy, Chaos, rolling his eyes.

There was silence from over the radio waves, and Noah watched out the window of his remote cabin as red and gold leaves from the blackjack oak spiraled wildly in a sharp gust of wind.

Fall was giving way to winter unseasonably early.

"I tell you the world is about to end, and I get a one-word answer?" Chaos' exasperation was obvious. "You're consistent, Mute. Over."

A rare smile threatened the corner of Noah's mouth.

His callsign as a Raider had been Mute. And after decades of serving together, Chaos knew him better than most. Noah was notoriously recalcitrant, and Chaos was one of the few people he trusted.

"This is serious, Mute. I know you're a self-sustaining hermit out there, but you should head into civilization to stock up on supplies. Over."

A sweep of apprehension had Noah's brow furrowing. His entire military career had been spent in the global fight against terrorism, but that was in his past. Now here it was, knocking on the door of his carefully isolated present.

Chaos had been picking up chatter coming from the CDC about the Syrian Virus—Sy-V—which, until a couple of hours ago, had been nothing more than rumors on the internet. Not that Noah was surfing the web—he didn't have telecommunications this far out in the wilderness of the Wichita Mountains.

Semi-regular contact with Chaos was the only connection to the outside world he needed. That, and making the trek into the closest small town every month for supplies.

As it had only been two weeks since he'd last made the arduous trip, he wasn't keen to head out again so soon. His insides shriveled a little at the thought of making small-talk and being in proximity to his fellow humans.

There was a reason he was living alone at the edge of the world.

"I'll touch base in a few days. Chaos, out."

"Mute, out."

Noah replaced the radio receiver carefully. Leaning back in his chair, he stared out the window, pre-occupied with running a virtual inventory of his provisions. He relied on solar power, with a diesel-run generator as backup, although he'd been meaning to convert the nearby stream into a source of energy—carrying gas cans in through the dense forest was a bitch.

His greenhouse provided vegetables year-round, and what meat he couldn't freeze from a hunt, he smoked.

While he regularly contemplated wringing the neck of his rooster, he was quite fond of the three hens who provided him with eggs, and he didn't think his pantry had the capacity for more storage of staples such as rice and flour. He had enough toothpaste and deodorant to last years, but he supposed he could always stock up on ammunition for his AR-15.

If anything was going to make him venture down the mountain, it was tobacco. If it really was the end of the world, he was damn well taking up cigarettes again.

NOAH GRUNTED when he finally reached his jeep, wiping at the perspiration on his forehead. While the air held a definite chill, he'd enjoyed pushing himself, testing his stamina and endurance. There were no roads into his secluded cabin, which meant he'd had to trek miles through difficult terrain to reach the thicket where he stowed his vehicle.

From here, it was a twenty-minute drive. He still wasn't convinced it was worth heading into civilization. Not when his shopping list comprised five items; long-life milk, coffee, crossword puzzles, cartons of cigarettes, and bullets.

None of them were necessities. Not even the ammunition. Once a Marine, always a Marine; his armory cupboard at the cabin was equipped to handle any contingency—even the apocalypse.

A keen awareness of the invisible threat of Sy-V underscored the usual unease that itched him as he entered town. Would the townspeople know what was coming? Would they already be sick?

Chaos had warned the rate of community transmission was so fast that the containment of Sy-V was basically impossible. Parking behind the mom-and-pop grocery store, Noah pulled on his heavy-duty winter gloves and tied a bandana around his face. Known as the Mountain Man, residents wouldn't look twice at his strange appearance.

It didn't take him long to get what he needed—bar the ammunition. He had a tweak of conscience seeing the customers jammed together at the one working cash register.

Grumblings indicated the store was short-staffed because of sickness.

An obligation to alert these people carelessly sharing oxygen warred with a deep-seated need to avoid any human interaction. He'd done his duty for his country, and now he had to trust the government would do its duty for their people.

A pregnant girl, little more than a teenager, began coughing, bending at the waist as the hacking left her breathless. Noah grimaced when the shoppers behind just pushed her forward in the line. He was grateful his reputation ensured people kept their distance.

With sharp eyes, he studied the people before him, recognizing the insidious signs of sickness in several: feverish eyes, panting breath, and harsh coughing.

The insistent urge to get far, far away had him unsettled. He clenched his teeth.

When it was his turn at the register, he flashed his basket and placed three fifty-dollar bills, easily double what his items cost, onto the counter before striding out. No way was he waiting for the products to be scanned and subjected to additional germs.

Fuck the ammunition. He was getting the hell out of there.

―――――

DAY 2

"ARE WE LOST?" Harper Daniels knew her petulant tone would piss her boyfriend off, but she was getting kind of pissed herself. To be fair, it was more at herself than him. She was a twenty-two-year-old woman who still couldn't say no. Hence, the never-ending trek to this "amazing spot" Samuel had been raving about when she'd rather spend her weekend curled up on the couch, reading.

The crisp air of the Wichita Mountains had been somewhat exhilarating when they had started out early that morning. With the fortification of caffeine, she had been low-key enthusiastic for the two-day camping trip Samuel had cajoled her into.

Several hours into the walk to their camping spot, she was less enthusiastic. The new hiking boots he had insisted on buying were rubbing at her heels, she really needed to pee, and she was eighty-seven percent sure Samuel had no idea where he was leading them.

"It's not too far now." Samuel stopped and turned to face her, forcing a smile. She could see the effort he was making and was suitably chagrinned.

She had agreed to come, so she needed to suck it up.

"I just need to, uh, relieve myself." She mentally grimaced at her awkwardness. She'd been dating Samuel for over a year now; it was ridiculous she couldn't say "pee".

This embarrassment was just one reason she kept dodging his suggestions that they move in together. Imagine living in such close quarters they could hear each other going to the bathroom?

She shuddered.

"Sure. Just don't go too far off," he cautioned, coughing as he uncapped a water bottle and drank deeply.

With a grateful sigh, Harper dropped her backpack to the ground, rummaging in a side-pocket for tissues. Standing, she rolled her shoulders, reveling in the sudden lightness. She swore the pack hadn't been this heavy when they'd started out.

Samuel was fiddling with a compass and map, absorbed in plotting his course through the wilderness.

Please, God, let him be right, and we don't have much further to walk.

Slipping into the dense foliage, she found a fallen tree trunk and crouched beside it, doing her business as efficiently as possible. To take her mind off the possibility of a creepy crawly biting her on the ass, she calculated how many times she'd be likely to do this in the next two days. She resolved to cut back on her water consumption.

She could handle being dehydrated for forty-eight hours.

NIGHT WAS FALLING when Samuel finally conceded defeat.

"We'll set up here." Hands on hips, he surveyed the small clearing they were standing in. "This might even be better than the spot I was aiming for."

Harper highly doubted that but kept her mouth closed. She'd happily set up camp anywhere, so long as she could stop walking and drink the champagne Samuel had brought —at the time, she'd wondered why he'd packed it. It had seemed out of character. For him, not for her. She believed any situation benefited from sparkling wine.

"Sure. What do you need help with?"

The sooner they were set up, the sooner she would be drinking.

"I can handle the tent. Why don't you—" He broke off, coughing violently. He'd had a cold for a day or two, and the cough was getting progressively worse.

"Are you feeling okay?" Harper was already rummaging through their small first aid kit, passing him some Tylenol.

"I just can't shake this headache."

Harper eyed him. He should really rest for a moment, but the encroaching darkness made getting up the tent a priority. What she wouldn't give to be sitting warm and cozy in her favorite armchair, reading HM Hodgson's latest fantasy romance.

Resolutely, she batted away the mental image.

"Here, let me..." She reached for the folded tent attached to the front of Samuel's pack.

"I said I had it!" Anger made his voice pitch high. Registering her surprise, he sighed. "Sorry. I'm frustrated. And feeling like crap. This isn't how I imagined our evening going."

"Well, we're here now. What can I do?"

"You could stop being so bitchy."

Harper's eyebrow twitched, and resentment rose in her chest, hot and consuming.

"How am I being bitchy?" Okay, that sounded bitchy.

"You've been hating this since we started out, and now you're blaming me for getting us lost."

"You *did* get us lost." And she thought she'd hidden her discontent better. "I'm just trying to be helpful."

The light was fading, and she didn't have the energy for this fight.

"Fine. Find some firewood, then." Samuel's lips pursed in that unattractive way he had. Like when she tipped valets, "it's their job", or she wore a skirt he deemed too short, "people will think you're a different kind of girl".

Tramping loudly through the undergrowth to scare away creepy crawlies, she snatched at random sticks and fumed. The problem was that she was exactly the kind of girl people thought she was, and she was okay with that.

Samuel was the one who wasn't.

He was continually smoothing at the edges of her impoverished background. She'd once joked to his boss that her mother had raised her and her sister on tips, and Samuel had laughed loudly and steered her away with a too-firm hand.

By the time she'd gathered an armful of firewood and returned to the clearing, he had erected the tent, and a small fire was flickering. He'd dragged a log over and was perched on it, pouring the champagne into two plastic flutes.

Accepting his silent peace offering, she put the wood beside the fire and took a seat beside him. She could already feel the bubbles on her tongue.

"Harper, you know I love you." He passed her a flute and put the other and the bottle on the ground at his feet. "I wanted to bring you out here this weekend to ask you an important question."

Blood drained from Harper's face, and her mouthful of champagne turned sour. She swallowed. And then swallowed again.

He wasn't... was he? No, surely not.

Struggling to one knee, Samuel pulled a small jewelry box from his pocket, his expression expectant.

No. No, no, no, no, no.

"Harper Felicity Daniels, will you be my wife?"

CHAPTER TWO

DAY 3

It was the bickering that first alerted Noah to the fact he had company. It was early morning, and he was out checking his snares when he heard them.

A man and a woman, packing up their campsite as they sniped viciously at one another. The guy sounded like a jerk and had a cough that marked him as a dead man walking.

Camouflaged in his natural habitat, Noah kept his distance and watched. The couple were uncomfortably close to his cabin, and he didn't want them any closer. He'd never had hikers come this far into the mountains.

The man fell against a log, coughing, and when he raised his head, Noah saw blood gushing from his nose.

Infected.

A stirring of pity had him glancing away. It was doubtful the two would make it back to civilization before they succumbed to Sy-V.

There was nothing he could do.

Scrubbing a hand over his beard, he turned away.

. . .

IT WAS JUST over a click back to his cabin, and the stillness of the day meant that the dropping leaves fell aimlessly. Peacefully.

Noah attempted to reclaim some of that peace.

Growing up, his grandfather's cabin had always been a retreat for him, remote and secluded. He'd known at the beginning of his last tour that he was done—he'd be leaving the Marines. This cabin was where he knew he needed to be. To find whatever peace was left to him in this world.

To have it compromised now, when so much was at stake, gave him an uncomfortable tightness in his chest. He lengthened his steps, keen to put as much distance between him and that couple as possible.

A faint scream rent the air, and his steps faltered.

It was the woman from the campsite. The fact he could hear her spoke to her desperation, and the hairs on the back of his neck prickled when the sound came again.

He stopped.

The suffocating dry heat of the desert replaced the cool mountain air as a tightly packed vehicle full of Afghani women and children drove over a mine and fractured into nothing but terrified, tortured screams.

Noah instinctively crouched, finding himself on the leaf-littered forest floor. Taking a deep breath, he forced his heart rate to settle.

Rising slowly, he started forward, only to halt again at more screaming.

Even as every tingling nerve ending in his body insisted he continue to the sanctuary of his cabin, he found himself heading back in the campsite's direction. He ratio-nalized the least he could do was explain what was happening; it was a fair bet the couple had no idea about Sy-V.

Reaching his previous vantage point, he assessed the situation. The man was lying in a crumpled heap on the ground, his face and the front of his shirt blood-soaked. The woman was sitting beside his unmoving body, rocking as she sobbed.

If the man wasn't dead, he was close to it.

Mindful of keeping his distance, he walked closer, purposefully making enough noise to catch the attention of the woman. Jerking her head towards him as he stopped at the edge of the clearing, she yelped in fright, jumping to her feet and backing away from him.

"Who are you?" Her voice was hoarse. Scared.

He held up a hand and made no move to approach her.

"I've got a gun," she threatened, her big eyes blinking furiously.

He highly doubted that. "I'm not going to hurt you."

"What are you doing here?"

"I heard you scream."

"Oh." She seemed to deflate, her terror dissolving. "I need help. My boyfriend... ex-boyfriend. He was sick, and then... now. He's dead." Her voice caught on a sob. "We're in the middle of nowhere, and I don't know how to get back, and I can't leave him here. What do I do?"

He studied her. She was a pretty little thing. Her flushed face could be from distress but was most likely the virus.

She wasn't coughing, though.

"Are you sick?"

"No. Why?"

He looked pointedly at the body and then back at her.

"He just had a cough and a headache. And then he

started bleeding and seizing and... You don't die from a cold. Maybe he got bitten by something?"

"There's a virus. It spreads fast, and it's deadly."

She took a step back from him.

"I don't have it." *But you probably do.*

She shook her head. "What are you talking about? What virus?" She narrowed her eyes and took another step back, the wariness having returned. "Why are you out here, anyway?"

"I live here."

"In the mountains?"

He nodded.

"By yourself?"

He nodded again.

"So you're some huge man-beast who lives alone in the mountains?" She bit her full lower lip. "Like that's not weird," she muttered to herself.

Something quirked within Noah, and he suppressed a smile.

"You should stay here," he said. "If you're infected, you don't want to spread it, and if you're not, you don't want to catch it."

"I can't stay out here!"

He shrugged. He didn't know what else to say.

And he'd already used up his allotment of words for the year.

Suspicion flared in her eyes, and she propped a hand on her hip. "There is no virus. You're doing the whole 'I've got a puppy in my van, come and see' trick."

He ran a hand over his beard. Chaos hadn't mentioned Sy-V making people delusional, but this woman clearly wasn't thinking clearly.

"You're going to kidnap me, aren't you? You're a serial

killer, and I'm going to end up on the six o'clock news, found hacked to pieces."

He blew out a breath.

"Before you abduct me, can I at least use your cell?"

He raised an eyebrow. The little harpy was amusing.

"The battery in my cell died. I need to call the authorities so they can come and get Samuel."

"I don't have a cell."

"Oh, my god. You really *are* a weirdo."

"There's no reception."

"Oh." Her hands twisted together. "I know you're not a serial killer. Sorry for saying that. I just... I don't know what to do."

Noah respected her caution. For all she knew, he *could* be a serial killer. He had the skills to be a damn good one.

"I'm going to go now." He knew that's what he needed to do. So why was he suddenly reluctant to leave her out here by herself?

"You can't go!"

"I can check on you tomorrow."

"I can't stay here. I have to get home. I need to call someone... 911, the police... Jesus, I don't even know who to call. Samuel's parents are going to be so mad at me. They never liked me. Can you believe he proposed last night? That's why we broke up." She ceased her rambling and just blinked at him.

"I'll come back tomorrow."

———

THERE WAS NOT a chance in hell Harper was going to stay here until tomorrow. She watched the man-beast slip back into the forest, soundless and far too graceful for a man of his size. He was *huge*. And intimidating, with that full beard, piercing eyes, and ragged scar down the side of his face.

Yep, she was out of here.

Grabbing at her backpack, she stuffed her sleeping bag inside, not bothering to roll it. Samuels' map and compass were in her pocket—she had no clue how to use either, but having them made her feel more in control.

Her gaze kept coming back to Samuel's body, and she finally gave in and approached him. She'd never seen a dead body in real life. A sob welled in her throat, but she pushed it down.

What if the man-beast was telling the truth? Had Samuel died from a virus? And if he had, did that mean she had it, too?

Last night had been indescribably awful. Samuel had been so shocked and angry when she'd turned down his proposal, and his scathing insults had cut deep. Between her guilt and her sadness, she'd been worried sick as his health deteriorated. She'd barely slept a wink, listening to his hacking cough and fevered breathing.

When he'd collapsed this morning, she thought he'd been bitten by something poisonous, a spider or snake. The swamping panic had held her immobile, and in those seconds of inaction, he had died.

She wanted to wipe the blood from his face but couldn't bring herself to touch him. Mercifully, his eyes were shut.

It felt wrong to walk away and leave him here alone. She unzipped his sleeping bag until it was flat and laid it over him, tucking the edges under his body.

She didn't know what else to do.

Looking around at the disorder of their campsite, she

picked up the unfinished bottle of champagne. It would be flat, but she didn't care.

Taking a swig from the bottle, she hoisted on her backpack and headed back the way they had come.

HARPER WAS LOST.

Really, truly, fucking lost.

Desperation pushed her on, fumbling through low-hanging branches and wincing as each step rubbed the raw blister on her heel. She'd finished the champagne, and now her mouth was tacky and dry, and fear was increasing her disorientation.

She had a thumping headache and, even though she knew it was stress and a lack of water, she couldn't help imagining an insidious virus creeping through her body.

What kind of virus could kill someone so quickly? She wished she'd paid more attention to the news. She'd heard of Ebola, but wasn't that just in Africa? Was it some kind of Avarian flu? Or was that man-beast just a delusional weirdo?

A sob escaped. She was never finding her way out of the wilderness. How long would it take her sister to realize she was missing and come looking? No doubt Samuel's parents would mobilize a massive search effort—she should try to find a clearing so a rescue helicopter could find her.

But not right now. Now, she needed to rest. She was tired. So tired.

Sinking to the ground, she used the pack on her back to lean against. She couldn't tell how far from the campsite she'd come. Everything looked the same out here. She was feeling lightheaded and finding it hard to concentrate, and oh god, she was going to die out here, and no one would ever know what had happened to her.

With a thick tongue, she licked her dry lips.

When she'd stopped drinking water yesterday to reduce her outdoor toileting, she hadn't considered the debilitating effects of dehydration.

She'd close her eyes, just for a moment, and when she felt better, she'd get moving again. Find a water source or a clearing. And help would come. If not for her, then for Samuel.

HARPER WAS ROUSED from a cottony blankness by something beside her. Something big.

Cracking an eyelid, she struggled to focus, and when she saw the man-beast crouched beside her, she squeaked and promptly closed her eye again.

If she couldn't see him, he wasn't real.

Could he hear her rapid heartbeat? She was so lethargic. Why was it beating so quickly?

There was a quiet huff, and then big hands were cradling her, lifting her. She squeaked again and screwed her eyes tighter still.

This wasn't happening.

She was not lying limp against man-beast's chest. His insanely muscled arms were not holding her tight, and she was not being carried back to his lair to be eaten. Or enslaved. Or tortured and then enslaved and then eaten.

She was just going to keep her eyes closed and pretend none of this was happening.

CHAPTER THREE

DAY 4

Noah hadn't thought about it. He'd just scooped her up and brought her back to the cabin.

He could have kicked himself for not bothering to bring a water canteen with him when he went out yesterday to check on the woman. When he found her, she'd been delirious, her rapid breathing and sunken eyes indicating dehydration.

She'd fainted in his arms, and although she'd woken enough when they'd arrived for him to feed her water, she'd crashed into a heavy sleep. No doubt exhausted from the stress and exertion... or from Sy-V.

Pacing before the couch he'd placed her on, he wondered for the thousandth time if he'd signed his own death certificate. He'd checked her temperature throughout the night, and every time the reading was normal, the band around his lungs eased some.

Each time, he ruthlessly crushed the spark of hope that kept flickering to life. He'd stayed alive through countless tours in the Marines; there was no way his luck was extending this far. Not with how Chaos had described the transmission and mortality rate of Sy-V.

He fished the cigarette packet from the pocket of his shirt and went to the front porch, keeping the door open so he still had eyes on the woman.

Breathing deeply of the nicotine, he sat leaning against the veranda post, drawing up a knee to prop his elbow on.

Focusing on the glowing ember of the cigarette, he absently flicked the ash. He'd promised his mother on her deathbed he'd give up, but he figured she'd understand the apocalypse was an acceptable exception.

What was happening in the world outside? He assumed all troops stationed overseas would have been recalled and, together with the National Guard, they'd be maintaining order in the cities and helping FEMA set up camps.

He'd tried getting in touch with Chaos last night with no luck.

A stirring on the couch caught his attention. She'd rolled onto her side, and her shirt had come untucked, revealing a smooth expanse of toned skin.

He quickly averted his eyes.

She was far too young for him to be noticing her in that way.

At thirty-five, he'd only had one serious girlfriend, and that was before he'd signed up. The military life wasn't conducive to relationships, and it wasn't something he'd ever wished for. He had his Marine buddies for companionship and had never found it difficult to keep his bed warm during R&R.

And this little harpy was definitely not his type. Regardless of the obvious age gap, she was too pretty and young and fresh.

And talked far too much.

The radio crackled to life, and Noah jumped to his feet, stubbing the cigarette out and striding to the desk set in the corner of the main room.

"CQ CQ CQ... this is Delta Foxtrot Zulu, standing by..."

Chaos.

Picking up the radio handset, Noah cleared his throat. "Delta Foxtrot Zulu, this is Alpha Bravo Whiskey... this is Alpha Bravo Whiskey, over."

"Mute. Did you get supplies? Over."

"Affirmative. Over."

"It's worse than I thought. The government is bombing entire cities to try to contain it, and telecommunications are down. Electricity won't be on for much longer. I heard a FEMA camp was over-run by rioters and all military radio channels are down. Over."

Noah's gut plummeted. He should be out there, helping.

"Don't even think about it, Mute." Chaos spoke into the silence, reading his mind. "Stay where you are. Over."

"Mindy? Over."

Mindy was Chaos' ex-wife, and their split was amicable enough that he was in Oklahoma City visiting her now.

"She, uh..." Chaos' voice cracked. "She didn't make it. Over."

Shit. Noah knew Chaos would be devastated, and his heart squeezed in sympathy.

"Are you sick? Over." Noah concentrated on stilling the slight tremble in his hand as he waited for his best friend's answer.

"Not yet. You? Over."

"Negative. Over."

"I'm bunkered down, for now. I've got rations for a week. Thought I'd make my way to the nearest base after that. Over."

"Get your ass here, Chaos. Forget the base. Over."

Static crackled over the radio waves.

"Okay. Yeah, okay, Mute. I'll start out tomorrow. Might take me a few days; most major roads aren't passable. Once I'm on the road, I'll have to rely on my high-frequency handset and local repeaters. Might not make contact until I'm close. Over."

Noah bowed his head, relief flooding his synapses.

"Stay safe. Over."

"You too, Mute. Don't leave the mountains; it's fucking crazy out here. Chaos, out."

"Mute, out."

The knowledge that Chaos was alive and making his way here had warmth radiating through his body. He had the insane urge to grin.

"Your name is Mute?"

Rolling his shoulders, Noah turned to face the woman, who was awake and alert. She'd pulled her knees beneath her chin and was watching him warily.

"It's Noah."

"The man on the radio called you Mute." Her eyes narrowed. "Which fits with the whole serial killer-vibe you've got going on. Why haven't you tied me up?" She raised slender wrists in the air, waving them at him.

He took a deep breath, unsure where to start. He'd saved the pocket-sized harpy's life, but from what little he knew of her, he wasn't expecting gratitude. He bit back a smirk.

"And now you've got your buddy in on the kidnapping?" Her eyes flicked to the radio behind him. "It's a little extreme, isn't it? Trying to convince me the world is ending and I can't go back to civilization. To be honest, he went a little heavy on the details. No one's going to believe the United States government is bombing their own cities. He would have been credible if he'd just dialed it back a bit. And what kind of name is Chaos? He's clearly watched too many Avengers movies."

"You're free to go."

"Of course you're going to say that. You probably want to watch me run and then hunt me down. And you've taken my boots, so there's that." She raised an eyebrow as though daring him to contradict her.

Getting up, he strolled to the open door and stood beside her boots, neatly lined up. Raising his own eyebrow, he turned away and went to the kitchenette, placing a water-filled kettle on top of the wood-burning stove.

He faced her, holding out two coffee mugs. "Coffee?"

She spluttered. "You're insane. Like, actually insane."

He turned to place one mug back on the shelf.

"Hold up there, man-beast. I'm not turning down caffeine. Jesus, you really *are* crazy."

With his back still to her, he grinned.

———

HARPER HAD NEVER LIKED Alice in Wonderland, and she liked the feeling of *being* Alice even less.

The man-beast was making her coffee in a cabin in the middle of nowhere.

Everything was upside down and nothing felt real. How had her life imploded so spectacularly? She should never have agreed to go on the stupid camping trip. That way, they would never have gotten lost. Samuel would never have proposed. They'd never have fought and broken up, and he'd never have...

A hollow pit bloomed in her stomach. Samuel was still out there. Alone.

"What is it?" Man-beast—Noah—was studying her, and Harper realized she was chewing her fingernails manically.

"Samuel's body..." Her voice hitched.

"I buried him." Noah continued making their coffee as though they were talking about a backyard project he'd just completed. "Do you take sugar?"

"You... what? You can't *bury* him. That's like, illegal. It's tampering with the scene of a crime. Well, not a crime. A death. The authorities need to investigate." She paused, grasping at the seven thousand thoughts that were crowding her brain. "When did you do this? *Why* did you do this? And yes, I like my coffee black with two sugars."

He paused and then dumped in two spoonfuls of sugar. She huffed. She hated when people judged her for her sugar addiction. Screw him and his chiseled, probably Paleo-induced, lean, muscled body. No one needed the pressure of that kind of perfection in their life.

She contemplated asking for three sugars just to see his reaction.

"Before I went looking for you. To protect his body from wild animals because the authorities aren't coming." He handed her a steaming mug, and she looked up, and up, into his face. He was the tallest man she'd ever encountered.

"Where?"

"Where did I bury him?"

"Yes! Where did you bury his body?" She clapped a hand over her mouth. "I can't believe those words just came out of my mouth. None of this is real, is it? I've been reading too many paranormal romance books, and I'm going to wake up at home and call Samuel and say, 'Sorry, I can't make that camping trip. I need to wash my hair that weekend. Oh, and by the way, I don't think we're right for each other and should break up.' And he's going to calmly accept my decision and wish me well."

Noah was standing frozen before her as though unable to comprehend her verbal diarrhea. "Do you want to pinch me, or should I do it myself? Never mind, I'll do it. Your hands are too big; you'll probably leave a bruise. Although, if this is a dream, I won't bruise, so there's that."

God damn, was she about to hyperventilate? She focused on the steam rising from her mug and calmed her breathing. In, and out.

"Harpy, you need to chill." He sat on the armchair opposite, his eyes trained on her.

"Harpy? It's Har-per. Harper." She furrowed her brow. "But I didn't tell you my name. How do you know my name?"

"I didn't. Harper, huh?" Amusement made a previously hidden dimple pop in his cheek.

"What's so funny? Have you been stalking me since before I came on this stupid trip?" She tilted her head, studying him back.

"I didn't know your name. I called you Harpy because you don't shut up."

"Well, that's just rude."

No need for him to know she'd been silently calling him man-beast. Or had she actually said it out loud? No matter.

She sipped at her coffee, the aromatic goodness soothing her. She wasn't actually afraid, which was strange in itself; she should be petrified, shouldn't she?

"How long do you think it takes for Stockholm Syndrome to kick in?" She went back to chewing on her fingernails. "And what do you mean the authorities aren't coming? There's probably a search party being organized right now. I should light a signal fire outside. Actually, that's much too passive. Why don't you just show me the way out of here, and I'll be on my way?"

He sighed. "You don't get it. The Syrian Virus has ended the world as you know it. If by some miracle you didn't catch it from your boyfriend—"

"Ex-boyfriend."

Another deep breath from man-beast.

"If you go back into town, you could catch it. And you will die." His tone was measured. Patient. "This is your best chance for survival."

Harper realized Noah believed the shit he was spouting. The poor man was a delusional recluse, and although he looked scary as hell, she was starting to suspect he was relatively harmless.

"So you never go into town?" Maybe he didn't know how to escape this end-of-the-world wilderness any more than she did. Which was depressing as hell. Imagine living out here for the rest of her life?

"Once a month, for supplies."

Hope jumped in her chest. Okay, they were getting somewhere.

"So, when is your next supply trip? I can tag along, and we can go our separate ways. Easy."

"No."

"No?"

"I'm not risking it. And neither should you."

Ugh. She gritted her teeth.

"So you want us to stay out here? Together? Forever?"

He stayed silent.

"Oh buddy, I am going to make your life so miserable,

you'll be carrying me back to civilization. I give you twenty-four hours before you're dropping me off at the welcome sign to town."

KEEP READING!
Ruined World

STAY IN TOUCH!

Want to read unedited chapters of my work as I write them? You can subscribe to my Patreon for just AUD$5/month!

♡ Exclusive first access to my books
♡ Receive chapters as I write them
♡ Provide comments and offer feedback

Check out my Patreon account: www.patreon.com/ JacquelineHayley

Keep up-to-date on what's happening with my email newsletter! You'll receive behind-the-scenes photos, romance memes, book reviews and other awesome stuff. (I am well aware "awesome stuff" is a broad term).

ABOUT

Jacqueline picked up her first Mills & Boon novel when she was fourteen, and fell head over heels in love with the romance of a happily-ever-after. *Sweet Valley High* just couldn't compete after she got hooked on dashing heroes and plucky heroines.

She has a Bachelor Degree in Print Journalism but, having always been tempted to embellish the facts of a story, decided she was more suited to writing works of fiction. She writes in between wrangling two daughters and her very own tall, handsome husband. *wink wink*

For more on Jacqueline, you can find her at:
    www.jacquelinehayley.com
    Facebook /jacquelinehayleyromance
    Instagram @jacquelinehayleyromance

Amazon
BookBub
Goodreads
TikTok
Pinterest

ALSO BY JACQUELINE HAYLEY

THE AFTER SERIES

Prequel (novella)

The Beginning of the End

Book 1

After Today

Book 2

After Yesterday

Book 3

After Tomorrow

Book 4

After The End

Printed in Great Britain
by Amazon

20586680R00147